ALTER
EGO

Tory Allyn

NOVELS
ALTER EGO*

*Book one in my series: THE DAVENPORT DECREES

Table of Contents

Chapter 1

Sirens echoed in the distance as Jack Stanwick entered the rural town of Rockfort, Virginia. Another gruesome discovery led the local boys to claim jurisdiction—but the Bureau had their own ideas and about to pull rank. After he sliced through the necessary red-tape and secured the needed sanctions, FBI Director Gordon Weaver issued an order to survey the tragedy and retrieve all remnants from Granite's Mill.

With hardly a resident looking his way, Jack hastened through the four-way stop and hurried up Old Gulch Road. He noticed the sparse trees had turned into a dense forest that dimmed an already cloudy sky. So after a quick flick of his wrist, the headlights came on.

As the car gained speed, it careened along the crushed- stone route. The loose gravel struck the undercarriage like a hail of bullets. At the same time, the screeching cry of police horns blared louder with each impending tread. It put him on high alert. While the adrenaline surged, he sped over a hill and caught sight of the glaring flares that inflamed his path, which improved his view. The crime scene now became visible.

Jack veered off onto a dusty road and pulled ahead of the pack of scattered cars. He shut off the engine, peered out the windshield and eyed the disarray of yellow police tape that encircled the crime scene. All the grave facial expressions gave weight to what lay just ahead.

Here we go again! His mind raced.

He reached over to unlock the glove compartment and removed a mini-recording device. Once his throat cleared, he pushed the corresponding buttons and spoke in a deep and sturdy voice, "This is Special Agent Jack Stanwick. It's Sunday, the twenty-sixth of October and the time is..." He looked at his watch then continued logging the rest of his statement. When finished, he unbuckled the seatbelt, shed his blazer and put on the regulatory FBI jacket.

Jack shoved the gadget into a pocket, turned it back on, and thrust open the door. He emerged from the car and was overtaken by a brisk wind that stiffened his face and stirred his spine. With a quick zip of his jacket, he advanced toward the group of men who had gathered around as if in a football huddle. One of the local cops approached him.

"You must be the FBI agent?" Out came a hand. "I'm Deputy Morton Talbot."

Jack grasped it. He noticed how the gun holster hung loosely around the deputy's waist; seemingly held up by a uniform that was one size too big.

"You got here mighty quick."

"I drove like a banshee." Jack turned and stuck his head between the congregated men. "Why is everybody just standing here?" He looked down at a body partially covered with leaves.

"We don't want to touch anything until Chief McAllister gets here."

Jack pulled out his head from the group. "Where is he?"

"The chief's on his way up from Gallagher County. He's been visiting his brother over the weekend." The deputy glanced at his pocket watch. "He should be here any minute."

Jack was raised to be respectful, but also knew cops from the South played by their own set of rules. If things weren't done their way, an investigation could come to a screeching halt and critical clues would be lost. "I take it you haven't started processing the crime scene? His eyes narrowed. "You know crucial evidence is disintegrating."

"Like I said before, we're waiting for the chief."

Realizing the jig—a name he called the dance—Jack prepared for another whirl. "Can't you initiate things?" He wanted to plant the seed. "Aren't you second in command?"

"Ah...yeah."

"Where's my CSI team?" "Right behind you."

Jack spun around his head and noticed some FBI vans from Quantico, Virginia.

"We've got our folks standing by," Deputy Talbot said. "I told your team that."

"C'mon people, you can at least take pictures." He pointed down. "I need those tire marks cast."

Nobody moved.

"Damn it!" His body wrenched. "Where's the camera?

I'll start this investigation myself."

"Oh no ya won't," bellowed a loud, crass voice. The man bustled his way through the crowd. "This here's my case that happened in my county that happened in my state."

Jack stood in the presence of the South's Wyatt Earp. He was a short, portly dynamo. Stuffed in an old suit with cowboy boots, he looked like a real hellcat. "You must be Chief Denton McAllister?"

"You'd be right, son."

"I'm FBI Special Agent Jack Stanwick." He stuck out his hand.

The chief ignored it, reached into his jacket pocket and pulled out a cigar. He bit off an end, ran it under his nose then popped the blunt into his mouth and lit it. His eyes darted

3

toward Deputy Talbot. "What's all this excitement about?" His heavy drawl languished. "Have ya found Jimmy Hoffa?"

A sharp burst of laughter erupted from his men.

"No," Deputy Talbot answered. "It's more like a freak show."

"I wouldn't call it that," Jack piped up.

The chief took a steady puff of his stogie. "I reckon I'll be the judge of that."

Jack gritted his teeth. These were backwoods boys and he knew nothing would get done if they weren't treated with kid gloves. "You know by all accounts the FBI would be taking over this case once we were informed." His voice remained calm and steady.

"I know the playbook, son." The fiery tip of Chief McAllister's cigar floundered with every word. "Your boss called the governor and raised a hell of a dickens."

"I don't know anything about that. What I do know is I've got to haul this body up to our medical examiner, and soon, so I need my CSI team to do their job."

The chief blew his noxious mist into the air. "Can I at least take a gander at the body before those fellas get in my way?"

"Just don't drop any ashes on the crime scene," Jack countered.

Chief McAllister clutched the cigar between his stubby fingers and stared him down. "Son, I've been doin' this here job a long time. Pert' near close to forty years now; about as long as ya been in swaddlin' clothes, and ya got the where-for- all to be tellin' me how to do my job?"

Jack didn't flinch. "No, sir, I wasn't."

The stogie slid back into his mouth. "I didn't think ya was."

Jack realized the conversation was going nowhere fast and that things had to be done differently. "Chief McAllister, I feel

4

we started off on the wrong foot. Look, I'm just here to oversee the investigation, grab whatever the CSI team finds and take the victim back to Washington, DC. That's it. I'm not here to step on any toes. Can we make this happen?"

The chief drew a lengthy hit off his cigar. "Ok, son, do what ya need." The smoke billowed out of a half-cracked smile.

Jack gestured to the CSI team to come out of their vehicles. "Thank you, sir." He slid on a pair of gloves.

"Yep." More smoke escaped out of his parted lips.

The CSI team walked up as Jack crouched down and brushed off the rest of the leaves from the body, careful not to disturb any evidence. After a quick inspection, he stood up and stared at Chief McAllister. "Go ahead, sir, take a look, but prepare yourself."

"Son, I've pert' near seen everythin'." He squatted down as much as his protruding gut would allow. "What in tarnation is this?" His breath rasped. "Where in God's creation did this thing come from?" Wheezing sounded. "Talbot, help me up."

The deputy grabbed onto the chief's hefty arm. "I told you it was freaky."

McAllister's eyes blazed. "This here some kinda joke..." He shifted around, his face flushed with fury. "Who's pullin' my leg?" His glare ended on Jack.

Agent Stanwick flung up his hands. "Look, I'm just down here doing my job."

"Show me them here credentials!" McAllister ordered. "I wanna make sure I'm not bein' taken a fool."

Jack reached into his back pocket, yanked out a leather case and flipped out his badge. "Here you are, Chief."

McAllister grabbed it, gave it a stern eye then handed it back. He faced Talbot. "I'm not amused."

The deputy stepped back.

Jack edged forward. Now that Chief McAllister had gotten a glimpse of his badge, the game had played out. It was time to enact his authority. "I'll tow the body away as soon as it's bagged and tagged."

"Boys, help the CSI gang process this here crime scene for the agent."

The men scrambled.

"I appreciate your help, sir." "Nothin' doin', son."

"Do you have any theories about the case?" Deputy Talbot inched in.

"It's too early to speculate," Jack responded.

The deputy snickered. "I think it's a tranny."

"A what?" Chief McAllister uttered.

"A transsexual, sir," Jack retorted. The chief's eyebrows crinkled.

"It's a person who has undergone gender reassignment surgery," Jack explained.

Deputy Talbot smirked. "Well, I call it what it is—a sex change."

Chief McAllister winced. "My God!" He turned both eyes heavenward. "One day this here sky's gonna open wide and when that happens y'all will witness His wrath."

A solemn expression emanated from Jack's face.

"Working the beat in Washington, DC, you come upon people like that," Deputy Talbot spoke up. "I've arrested drag queens and transsexuals for all kinds of things, especially prostitution. They're out on the streets selling favors right along with the real women…"

"I've come across a few of them myself," Jack added.

"I remember one case in particular," continued the deputy. "My partner and I had pulled up to a red light in an unmarked car when we noticed this beautiful woman hustling on the corner. We watched as a guy strolled up and struck a conversation with her. Within a couple of seconds, this guy was throwing punches while she was kicking back; slamming him in the head with her purse. We stormed out of the car, arrested both and tossed them into the backseat. They still fought; calling each other out. She was yelling that he was a pimp, and he was hollering that she was a man. When we got back to the station, we found out that she was indeed a man. I was shocked. I mean, she was hot; looked like a model. I knew right then and there that the big city had run its course. I needed to move to a small town where a woman was actually—a woman."

Jack shook his head. "I don't think this person is a transsexual."

"Then it's one of those um..." Chief McAllister snapped his fingers. "I've seen 'em on the ol' television with the missus. It's a her, um...a herm, a..."

"A hermaphrodite," Jack pronounced.

"Yep, one of those things," the chief said.

"No, the victim isn't a hermaphrodite," Jack remarked. "Usually they're born with both male and female genitalia as one sex, either a man or a woman. This body's a mixture of male and female features. Determining the original sex could be quite a challenge."

"Well, I think it's disgustin'," Chief McAllister clamored. "All these new fads creepin' 'round out there and the drugs these here young-uns are taking. No wonder there's creatures like this roamin' the planet. My missus is worried about our grandkids, especially with these bath salts and whatever else is here slitherin' down the ol' pipeline."

"We just had to arrest a teen the other day for arson." Deputy Talbot rattled his handcuffs. "This kid snorted some industrial-strength glue that was stored in his parent's garage and thought the Devil was in the house. So he grabbed his dad's welding torch as a weapon and went after him, burning down the house in the process. The boy was clearly out of his mind."

"Times are certainly changing." Jack nodded. "Years ago you didn't see drugs in the sticks. It's now moving from the city streets to the suburban sidewalks."

"Right into our own backyards," Deputy Talbot blurted out. "It seems these kids nowadays will sniff, snort or swallow just about anything for a high. Right, Chief?"

"Enough with the darn yappin' 'bout that!" McAllister's head bowed toward the body. "Somethin' fishy is goin' on here. If it's not one of them there hermaphrodites then what in God's graces is it?"

"They just turned over the victim." Jack nudged in to get a glimpse.

"I also want to see it." Talbot eked his way in.

Jack leaned in for several minutes then backed out. The deputy followed.

"What did y'all see or hear?" McAllister asked.

"I didn't see any contusions, lacerations, blunt trauma or strangulation, which I heard confirmed," Jack reported. "The CSI agents are just now looking for fluids and anything latent," he mentioned. "Besides obvious rigor and pooling, the only unusual thing I observed was the combination of male and female characteristics. It's like a morphing of sorts took place."

"A what?" Chief McAllister uttered.

"It's as if you took two bodies of the opposite sex and mashed them together, making them into one." Jack squashed his hands against one another. "It's called morphed or morphing. It comes from the word metamorphoses."

"Y'all and ya big city words." The chief shrugged.

8

"It basically means the changing from one entity into another," Jack explained. "You know when a caterpillar changes into a butterfly. That's metamorphosing one thing into another."

Chief McAllister's head pitched back. "Now, I've done gotcha."

A vehicle roared up and parked a few feet away. The faint sound of country music seeped out of an open window.

"That's Macdonald Cole, the Rockfort County Coroner." Deputy Talbot grinned. "He's a real character."

The coroner jumped out of his car and rushed up to them.

"Hi, Mac."

"Hey, Chief." Cole slapped him on the shoulder. "Sorry about being so late. Old lady Winslow finally died so I was out to her house. Things would've gone smooth if it wasn't for that touched son of hers getting in my darn way. You know his nonsense. He kept babbling that her soul was sucked out by some aliens from a planet I've never even heard of. Those damn aliens should've sucked him instead."

Chief McAllister sniggered under his breath as he reached an arm around Cole. "Well, this here'll make your day."

"I heard it's something out of a circus sideshow." Mac looked down at the body and leapt back. "Phew, what happened here?"

"I'm afraid we've got more than a sideshow on our hands!"

Chief McAllister moved in. "This here's Special Agent Stanwick with the FBI."

Mac lobbed out his hand as Jack halfheartedly took it. "I see you're using the forensic team from Quantico."

Jack pulled away. "Yeah."

"What're you here for?" Mac asked.

"For taking over our case," Deputy Talbot responded.

Mac eyed Jack. "Then why'd you call me?" "I didn't."

Mac pulled forward his baseball cap. "I should explain something."

"Go ahead." Jack stood focused.

"I've been in this business a long time and have seen many a corpse so I tend to take things with a grain of salt, and sometimes it rubs people the wrong way. I feel that might've happened here."

"Don't worry about it." Jack loosened his stance. "I'm somewhat tense myself. It's not every day where you see a victim who is a morphed mess of male and female parts."

"If it helps, I've never seen this muddle of hodgepodge either." Mac gestured with his head. "I should see if those agents need any help."

"Thanks, I'd appreciate that." Jack nodded. "As soon as the CSI team gets finished processing the crime scene, I'll be taking the body back with me to Washington, DC, to reunite with the others."

Gasps were heard.

He slipped, and they caught it.

Mac's eyes widened. "Did you just say—others?"

"There's more?" Deputy Talbot asked.

Jack huffed. "Listen, what I'm about to say needs to stay close to the vest. I don't want the press to catch a word. They'll just muddy the waters while fishing for a tale to tell."

Heads shook in agreement.

"Son, just how many others did ya find?" Chief McAllister questioned.

"Two bodies were discovered in Maryland over the weekend, and now this one."

Deputy Talbot pointed down to the victim. "Do they look like him, ah...her, um...that?"

"Yeah." Jack peered down at the body. "All have those disturbing male and female characteristics."

"Chief! Chief!" A young man ran up. "Jay, what's with the dang racket?" "We've found another body."

"Where?" McAllister roared.

"Down yonder, right behind Granite's Mill."

They bolted down the hill toward the old stone structure. In the distance, the warped paddlewheel wobbled from the weight of the cascading currents.

Jack arrived first, followed by Deputy Talbot and Macdonald Cole.

"Don't ya boys touch nothin' till I get there, do ya hear me?" McAllister hobbled down the hill. He rounded the corner and slowed to nearly a crawl. The chief was winded. "Is it another, um...he/she?"

"He's not altered at all," Jack noted.

Chief McAllister removed the cowboy hat and wiped off his bald dome. He placed it back on, shoved the damp handkerchief into a pocket and looked down.

"Do you know him?" Jack asked.

"Beats me who this here fella is." Chief McAllister shrugged. He turned to his men. "I want y'all to fan out and search a hundred yard radius of both these crime scenes. Could be some more bodies settin' along."

Jack turned to the chief. "Do you mind if I..." He pointed down. "Check him out?"

"Nah, go for it, son."

Jack put on a fresh pair of gloves and lifted a side of the body. While his eyes ran up and down, he patted every inch. Raising the other side, he completed the same routine and got up.

Deputy Talbot leaned in. "What's in your hand?"

"His wallet." Jack opened it. "According to a Social Security card, he's Harvey Welch."

"I don't recognize the name," Mac said.

The other men shook their heads in agreement.

Jack rifled through it. "Other than a little cash and some betting stubs, there's nothing else in it."

"Talbot," Chief McAllister grunted. "Grab an evidence bag."

Mac leaned in. "I wonder who he is?"

"At least he's a guy," Jack quipped. "My pat job confirmed that."

"I better go over and tell those agents they have more work to do," Mac offered. "I'll be back in a jiffy."

A young man walked up to the chief. "Sir, we've gone over the first victim and the surrounding area with a fine-tooth comb. The Quantico team has the bagged contents, impressions, castings and whatnot. They're ready to process the second scene."

"Good work, Boyd."

"Here's a few evidence bags." The young man handed them off. "Deputy Talbot said you needed these as he took off into the woods to relieve himself."

"That Morton has the bladder size of a small critter." Chief McAllister mocked. He keeps a small bottle of that there hand sanitizer in his back pocket just for situations like these." He laughed. "Well, Boyd, we're gonna get outta the way so y'all can do your work."

The young man smiled.

Chief McAllister gave Agent Stanwick an evidence bag as they headed up the hill.

Jack dropped the wallet in and sealed it. "You've got a really tight team."

"Yep, took me some time though, whoopin' these strappin' young boys into shape. Let's just say it aged me a few years, but we've pert' near got it down to a science."

"Would you come up to DC, and teach my partner a thing or two?"

"I reckon a cracking of the whip is in order."

"I'll keep your number in my book—just in case."

Mac walked up to Jack and handed him a piece of paper. "I did a liver temp on both bodies for an estimated time of death. They most likely spent the night here," he remarked. "I put it beside their names. The first one I called Mrs. Doe. It's Mr. and Ms. added together, and the second is HW, obviously for Harvey Welch."

"Thanks." He bared a slight grin. "Would you do a favor for me and ready the bodies for transport when the CSI agents have finished? My team should be here any minute."

"Your men pulled up when I put my instrument bag in the car, but I'll still help prepare them," Mac replied. "I'm just happy as a pig in slop not having to open those two up, especially the first one," he clamored. "Well, boys, see you around."

They watched him trot away as Deputy Talbot strode up.

"You're both right..." Jack chuckled. "He's something all right."

"More like something else," Deputy Talbot added.

Chief McAllister snickered. "Ya gotta be a certain breed to be a coroner."

Nodding and laughter took over.

"Well, gentlemen, I better get over to the transport vehicle and help. I don't want it to look like I'm slacking." Jack held out his hand. "Thanks for your cooperation."

Deputy Talbot grasped the offered hand. "You're welcome."

Jack extended his hand to the chief, but instead of taking it he pulled out a cigar, ran it under his nose and inhaled the smell. Agent Stanwick immediately pulled it back, tilted his head and winked an eye. Chief McAllister grinned then fired up his lighter.

"By the way, son, how'd ya agency find out about this here crime?"

"I phoned the Bureau," Deputy Talbot responded. "You did leave me in charge. Besides, I couldn't get you on the radio or your phone."

Jack watched as Chief McAllister turned his head toward Talbot. "Ya did, huh?" A slight smile gave way. "Good work, Deputy."

His eyes shined.

"I almost think here you're gunnin' for a raise," the chief continued.

"Yes, sir," Deputy Talbot stated. "You taught me well."

"I'd say I did."

Jack stepped back, admiring Chief McAllister. He knew that was the way to treat your squad—with commendation.

"Well, Talbot, enough yammerin' about this nonsense, I've gotta talk a minute to Jack. Why don't ya run over and help Mac with...well, everythin'?"

The deputy hurried away and called out a hasty goodbye.

Jack glanced at Chief McAllister and noticed his expression had shifted.

14

"I just can't reckon the idea that this kinda thing would happen in my jurisdiction. I've lived in these parts all my life and have never come across anythin' of this sort. The only body I've seen in a while is when ol' Joe Hubbard shot himself while deer huntin' a couple years back." He rubbed his chin. "I know somethin' though. These here boys at the ol' precinct are gonna have a field-day over this yarn."

"Would you wait until I get a better grasp around this case before you give the press all the details?" Jack requested. "I don't want the media getting wind of this and blowing all over us for answers."

"Gotcha," Chief McAllister uttered. "I'll make mighty sure to lay down the law. It'll all stay hunkered down."

"I really appreciate your help," Jack remarked. "I might need more of it in the near future."

"Just give me a holla."

"I know we started off on the wrong foot but, um...I..."

"Son, I know. No need here to mention it."

"Thanks, sir."

"Just let me know how everythin' turns out?"

"I will, and if you hear anything pertinent, you'll let me know."

"You betcha!" Chief McAllister tipped his hat. "Well, I guess it's pert' near time for me to be takin' my hide and high-tailin' it out of Dodge. It's not like I got me a precinct to run." He looked about then thrust out his hand. "Bye, son."

Jack, thrown off-guard, reached out and grabbed it. He gave a quick shake then let go. "Goodbye, Chief."

McAllister dipped his head then toddled away as the cigar smoke trailed behind him.

Chapter 2

*A*nother body found, somebody's loved one. *Now Harvey Welch has entered the picture. What's his role in all of this?* Jack looked on as Chief McAllister and Deputy Talbot drove off, followed by Macdonald Cole and both CSI teams. After walking over to the primary crime scene for one last look, he stood silent and glanced at the bleeding autumn leaves falling against the ground with crisp jabs. It reminded him that winter was just around the corner. The smell of wood-burning fireplaces only enhanced the effect.

As he bent down to get a closer look, Jack sensed these crimes couldn't be mere coincidences. The gut kept nagging him about that. His thoughts drifted back to what an old sergeant once told him. *'Always follow your gut instinct. Your first reaction is the best one so trust it. If you stop to think or second guess yourself it could have grave consequences.'* Jack picked up some leaves and examined them as if they held the clues to the strange bodies. *How many more graves will there be?* He stood up, threw the colorful objects into the air and stepped away.

Jack walked up to the car, slid behind the wheel and adjusted the mirror to see the transport team behind him. He pulled the cell phone out of his jacket pocket and dialed his partner's number. After seven years together, they'd never failed each other. Blaine knew what steps to take next.

"Federal Bureau of Investigation, Special Agent Michaels speaking."

"Hey trouble, it's Jack. What're you up to?"

"I'm sifting through the paperwork on the Yarborough case, and there's a ton of it."

"There always is." Jack watched his men climb into the transport vehicle. He was ready to leave.

"There wouldn't be if I had someone's help!"

"I headed for your desk, but instead caught this case. Anyways, Weaver knows you're better at documenting and I'm better with the grunt work."

"Director Weaver told you this?"

"Not in so many words, but I can feel it in my gut." Jack started the car. "Weaver always comes to me with a case and always says how orderly your reports are. It's just an assumption."

"It's more like he bumped into you first," Blaine stated. "Just one time I'd love to swap jobs and see what gives."

"Well, I can't today. You know how Weaver gets when we don't have those reports finished."

"When has it ever been—we?"

"Next time we'll switch it up a bit."

"I'll be old, hunched over and bald by the time that comes a calling."

The transport team flashed their high beams, indicating they were ready to leave. Jack shifted into drive and maneuvered through the grass to the gravel road. The team followed.

"In the meantime, put a rush on that paperwork so you can jump on this case. I'm calling for all hands on deck."

"Is that a cry for help?"

"It's more a plea for support."

Blaine chuckled. "Hold on a second…"

As Jack approached a stop sign, he lowered his window to get a whiff of the country air. To his left stood the Rockfort General Store, where a handful of men sat in rocking chairs. A jug of sustainability was lifted to a thirsty tongue while the others freely smoked their tobacco pipes. Regaling stories high and low were the order of the day.

"I'm back," Blaine said. "I got some Afro Sheen on the receiver and had to wipe it down. Just started using it."

"Afro Sheen! Who're you trying to look good for?"

"There's no trying involved. I look real good for the ladies."

Jack enjoyed teasing Blaine. They've been together longer than both of their dating streaks combined. The constant barbs kept the friendship strong and on point.

"So you didn't start wearing it for me?"

"Definitely not!" Blaine taunted. "But there's one thing I've definitely been doing besides form-filling, and that's wondering where you've been all day."

"I've been in Rockfort all day, and having a crazy one at that." Weariness leaked out of Jack's voice. "I left you a note. Didn't you see it? I slid it under your paper-clip thingamajig where I always do."

"You expected me to translate your chicken scratch. Even our handwriting tech would've had trouble deciphering it."

"Enough, I get your point!" Jack passed a slow-moving tractor. "Next time, I'll write it in longhand."

"So what's all the hoopla in Rockfort, since I didn't get a heads-up from anybody?"

"Another body, and it's deformed like the others."

"Are you serious?"

"Dead serious! But that's not even the best part."

"What? Tell me."

18

"A second body was found."

"Really?"

"Yeah, and get this, he was all male and had on clothes," Jack retorted. "From what I could see, and feel, there were no female parts anywhere."

"Wow, that's strange."

"It's what we usually deal with."

"Isn't that the truth?"

"Truth is, this psycho could be playing some sort of demented, ritual game."

"Crazy to play games with us."

"Right!" Jack turned on his high beams. "It's so dark out here, and I haven't seen a house for five miles."

"I could never live out in the boondocks. I'd much rather hear children than chickens."

"On that note, have you heard from Missing Persons?"

"I've got the reports sitting right here."

"Just give me a quick overview," Jack instructed. "I'm not in the mood for a dissertation. I'm already falling asleep at the wheel."

"Who do you think I am—Agent Trayber?"

"Yeah, that's all I need. I swear every time Trayber speaks it sounds like he's reading a phone book."

"Ok, but you're being forewarned, I'm going to tear through them," Blaine uttered.

"That's fine with me. Tear away!"

"The first victim, a 48-year-old male named Hal Bennett, was a construction manager working on the site of a new hotel. The report states that Hal called his wife that evening saying he'd be late for dinner. When he didn't come home, the wife became worried and informed the police."

"Yeah, who wouldn't?"

"The second, a 52-year-old male named Carter Reyes, was a security guard on the night watch at a local mini- mart. According to the clerk at the store, Carter told her he was going outside for a smoke, but never came back. The clerk telephoned the police, and, like the first victim, the body was found shortly thereafter. Both of them, as you know, were recovered in that unexplainable condition."

"Oh, I know." Jack peeked in his rearview mirror to see if the transport team kept pace. "Wait until you get a gander at this beauty."

"No thanks!"

"Was there anything else?"

"I did some further digging to see if I could link victim one and victim two together, but nothing showed up," Blaine answered. "They didn't know each other, their employment paths never crossed nor had they met socially. There was no connection between them."

"Strange deaths seem to be our forte."

"Remember the Horoscope Hitter?"

"The media named him that," Jack responded, playing the scene out in his mind. "That case still bothers me."

"It bothered a lot of people, especially the parents of the murdered girls."

"I still can't believe the way that psycho did them." The scumbag pummeled their body's postmortem and staple-gunned the month's astrological sign to each victim's blouse.

"Smearing his bloody fingerprints gave it a nice touch," Blaine added.

"Oh, for sure!"

"He was messing with us."

"Don't they all?"

"Yeah, thank God we had some help from the Davenport Detective Agency." Jack's thoughts again strayed back. "I was so glad they entered the picture."

"They were amazing! And if I got this right, one of them was the murdered victim's cousin."

"You got it right—for once."

"Oh, that's how you're going to play me?"

"Just releasing some pent-up aggression," Jack stressed. "It was great how the guys came in and helped us with the investigation."

"Man, they ran with it."

"All the way to the courthouse."

"Yeah, it must've been hard sitting in the gallery each day listening to every gory detail," Blaine noted. "I guess it was worth it when the jury handed down their verdict and the judge delivered the sentence. The death penalty devoured him up."

"Deservedly so."

"Good riddance to bad trash! That's what my momma used to say."

Jack chuckled.

"I'm glad you laughed, because now comes the fun part."

"No way!"

"I've got some news to deliver."

"What kind of news?"

"Well, it depends on what you'd rather have first," Blaine offered. "The bad news or the really bad news?"

"Oh, great!" Jack huffed. "Give me the bad news first."

"Are you sitting down?"

"No, I'm wind-surfing on the roof of my Buick!" Jack's voice ascended an octave. "As a matter of fact I just pulled up the north onramp of I-95, and of course as always it's swamped."

"Well, I was just trying to lighten a tense situation."

"I appreciate that, but in my mood just give it to me straight." He knew waiting wasn't going to help.

"I'm hearing that Carlton Woodbine, the only child of Virginia's Governor Jonathan Woodbine, had gone missing a few hours ago."

"You're kidding." Jack struggled to process the news. "Are you sure of this?"

"Well, I guess. I mean, I haven't seen anything official, but I've heard about it."

"Exactly what've you heard?"

"Marge, Weaver's secretary, told me she had heard about Governor Woodbine's phone call, but it's just hearsay."

"She's into you. Is that who you've been wearing the hair stuff for?"

"Oh, you're taking me there now! She's old enough to be my mother."

Jack crowed out loud. "Thanks, I needed that."

"What're friends for?"

"They're for telling me the gist of this grapevine."

"Supposedly, Carlton went to a party Saturday night and never came home. According to his parents, they contacted his friends and family and so far nobody has seen or heard from him. I hear his father is beside himself, but the mother, guess she's a real piece of work."

"Just what I needed to hear."

"Oh, wait, it gets much better."

"Damn it!" Jack laid on the horn. "Some hole just cut me off. I've half a mind to pull him over and give it to him."

"I hope you don't give the half you use."

"What?"

"You've got a little road rage going on."

"When I get a hold of him, it'll be going off."

"Just let it go. Besides, I've still got the really bad news to tell you."

After he took a deep, steady breath, Jack let it out. "Go ahead. I think I'm ready."

"I've also heard through the same vine that the Bureau wants you to interview the family and help them with their upcoming press conference."

"Damn it! Damn it! Damn it!" His voice rose louder with each exclamation. "Are you kidding me?"

"Wish I was."

"That's the worst part of this job." He slammed his hand on the steering wheel. "Dealing with family members—it's not my thing, especially when you've got to tell them a loved one is missing—or worse—dead. Damn it! Why don't they get Trayber to do it? He loves being the bearer of bad news. He's much more suited for this mission."

"Agent Trayber is in New York City with the others. They're handing down indictments on the Carmini crime family as we speak. You know they've had them under surveillance since last year, and from what I've been privy to, things are going down fast and the agents could be stuck there awhile. You've got the grand jury, testimony, closing arguments, and then waiting for that all- encompassing verdict. They'll probably still be there long after our case is solved."

"Again, not what I wanted to hear," Jack uttered. "I swear it goes from bad to worse. Who else can we bring in on the case?"

"The rest are spread quite thin."

"What about Grosso, Jablonski, Meltzer, Parsons—"

"They're helping with the Counter-Terrorism unit," Blaine interjected. "The jihadists have threatened to blow up the two biggest malls—the Mall of the Americas in Bloomington, Minnesota, and Destiny, USA in Syracuse, New York. I've heard they're plotting more targets from churches to corporations. They want to level our institutions so the more agents they have the better. Between ISIS, Al-Qaida and these other rebel factions gaining steam, they've got their hands full."

"I certainly agree, but there has to be some floaters."

"They've floated past our department after you've alienated them."

"Me!" Jack squawked. "How do you figure that?"

"By calling some of them utter morons when you directed a training mission."

"They were!"

"That may be the case, but you don't degrade them in front of their comrades."

Jack exhaled. "Where's Aiken, Bigelow and Layton?"

"They also have floated right by because somebody told them they were brain-dead, and not to bother sending them to a scientific institution when they're dead because they all have a disease called nincompoops."

"Yeah, well I wouldn't train any of those jarheads anyways."

"Ah, that's because you've been banned from training any new recruits."

"Good! Just because they've been trained to kill by our Marine Corps doesn't give them the knowledge on doing field work for the FBI," Jack groused. Last year, when you had the flu..."

"Don't remind me. I was sick for over three weeks. I thought for sure it was mad cow disease."

"I worked with one that had mad sow disease. Every time I'd turn around this guy was slopping down some food. He nearly cleaned out our vending machines. It was better to let him go hog wild while I worked up the case."

"Looks like you're stuck with me from now on."

"It sure looks that way.

"Oh, before I forget, I've requested Carlton Woodbine's dental records just in case," Blaine issued. "They should be at the Medical Examiner's office by morning."

There was total silence.

"Jack?"

"Huh?"

"Carlton's dental records."

"What about them?"

"You're not even listening to me," Blaine retorted. "Are you in one of your intestinal moods?"

"It's called a gut feeling."

"And what's it feeling?"

"What if this third victim is Carlton Woodbine?"

"Are you serious?

"Dead serious!" Jack reacted.

"I was just following standard protocol when asking for his dental records."

"So you never felt they might be Carlton's."

"Maybe once, twice at the most, but only when I spoke to the dentist."

"You should try feeling it all day!"

"So, somewhere in your gastrointestinal tract there's this notion brewing that Carlton is the disfigured body found down in Rockfort?"

"That's what my gut's telling me, and that's not all..." Jack couldn't shake the tension in his entire body. "Now with this third body resembling the other two, these victims aren't just coincidences. I felt this before and I was right."

"You rely heavily on that old instinct of yours."

"Yeah, I've honed it." His voice became steadily alert. "When I was a beat cop on the streets, I saw a lot, but nothing this bizarre. I mean, these deaths are outlandish. Way out there. I keep asking myself, who'd do something like this? You've got to be really sick or hell-bent sinister to try and pull this off." Jack shuddered. *This freak could be striking a person at this very moment.* He breathed out.

"Ah, you there?"

"Yeah, didn't mean to ramble on. I've got so many questions and getting so little answers. Guess I'm just tuckered out for one evening."

"You didn't just say the word—'tuckered'?"

"Man, I sound like Chief McAllister."

"Who?"

"Nothing."

"It sounds like you've been in Virginia too long."

"Yeah, way too long," Jack added. "Once I get this body on ice, I'm heading home to get some sleep. I suggest you do the same. Tomorrow, we'll be hopping."

"Or hopping mad, depending on the information we receive."

"Speaking of that, we need to make sure the press isn't a step ahead of us." Jack knew what those consequences could be. "If word gets out about the disappearance of the Governor's son, it could cause a media frenzy and that's something we don't need this early on in our case."

"Or this late in an election year."

"Wow, thanks for the reminder."

"What're partners for?"

"Not for that kind of update."

"I hear you."

"Go home. Get some sleep."

"Now you're talking!" Blaine agreed. "Adios."

"Arrivederci." Jack shut off the phone and led his team to the morgue.

Chapter 3

Like clockwork, the alarm sounded its almighty wake-up call at 7:00am. Jack, groggy from a restless night, rolled over and turned off the trumpeting noise. He climbed out of bed, threw on a bathrobe and roamed toward the kitchen for his morning routine. While the coffee brewed, he went out the front door to fetch the newspaper.

"Hello, birthday boy!" came the shrieking screech.

No way! It's nosy Mrs. Benson from across the street.

"Hi, Harriet," Jack shouted. "You get me every year."

"I cannot believe you're forty-two. Why, I remember you as a little boy, climbing up the oak tree in my front yard. Your mother, God rest her soul, would have been so proud of the way you turned out. Such a dashing young man, and working for the FBI! Now we just have to find you a suitable wife..."

"Harriet," Mr. Benson hollered. "Leave that poor boy alone. Get back in here and stop all that cackling. He doesn't want the whole neighborhood hearing that nonsense."

"For goodness sakes, Alfred, they already know."

"Bye, Mrs. Benson." Jack eased back inside.

"Goodbye, dear," came the shrill response.

He shut the door, put the back of his head against it and breathed out. Except for Blaine, nobody at the office knew and he wanted it that way. All the fuss—who needs it? That was his motto.

Jack brought the air back into his lungs and smelled the lingering aroma. He poured a cup, sat down at the table and took a sip. With a robust yank, the newspaper came out of the plastic wrapper and opened to the front page. There in bold print appeared the heading: Son of Virginia's Governor Disappears—accompanied by a picture of Carlton Woodbine.

What? Jack couldn't swallow it. *Who could've talked?* He peered at the photo of Carlton shaking President Dickson's hand. The kid won something that a rich family's child usually wins, especially one who has a governor for a father. But Carlton didn't resemble, in any way, the nude body at Granite's Mill. Even so, Jack felt it was him. He hopped up, scrambled to the phone and dialed.

"Hello."

"Have you seen today's headline in the Washington Tribune?"

"Just read it," Blaine replied. "I was about to call you when…"

"How could the press have already gotten wind of this?" Jack huffed. "I'm sure the governor wanted it kept in- house."

"Maybe the police down in Virginia tipped them off. After all, they're probably a bunch of local yokels with alliances to nobody."

"Chief McAllister told me he was going to hunker down the press."

"'Hunker down'—is that what you just said?"

"It's a southern thing." Jack evaded the question. "Just let it go."

"Maybe we've got our own mole."

Jack paced back and forth. "You mean a rat." He tried to grasp the enormity of what had taken place.

"How're we going to keep a lid on this case now? Every newspaper will run this story front and center, not to mention the news stations. People are now waking up to it on the internet."

Jack slammed the paper against the table. "Thanks to this reporter." He leaned over and zeroed in on the name.

"Are you there?"

"Yeah, the byline calls her Simone Wellington." He focused on her face and saw how pretty she was.

"She's pretty..."

"What?"

"She's pretty good," Blaine continued. "Very informative. I read her column in the morning on the commode."

"Ooh, man."

"Sorry, that was too informative."

Jack shook it off. "I need to get ahead of this woman."

"Instead of being behind her."

"That reminds me, we need to haul butt on this case before the mass media monstrosity is on our tails."

"Or the District Attorney, and you know she likes your tail."

"Yeah, let's not remind me about DA Griswold."

"No reminding here."

"After I call this reporter, I'm jumping in the shower then going over to see if Edgar Cromwell has anything to tell me about the latest victim. I'll be at my desk after that."

"I'm ready to walk out the door as we speak."

Jack sneered. "Don't forget your Afro Sheen!"

"Really, you're now going to take me there?"

"If I wasn't so pissed I'd be plenty laughing."

30

"Speaking of plenty, there's still a lot of paperwork left on the Yarborough case. Feel like laughing now?"

"Point taken!" Jack enunciated both words. "Could you do a huge favor for me and forgo working on that case to help with crowd control? I can't do both. I've mentioned to Weaver he should hire a consulting firm for that."

"Yes, there should be a more professional liaison between us and the reporters, especially when something horrible happens to a governmental bigwig or their family."

"It would certainly give us more time to maybe...solve the case."

"That'd be nice."

"Well, in the meantime, try to keep a lid on this boiling pot without sounding like you're beating around the bush. Give it your diplomatic charm."

"Always eager to please!"

"Please them," Jack emphasized. "Reporters don't want to hear anything vague. They want the full scoop. They'll sniff out a story a mile away and we can't give them a scent. Nothing scandalous can break out at this point in time. Not with it being a reelection year. That's all we need."

"Don't worry! I'm very good at a cover-up."

"Oh, you're funny. Leave your comedic side home and get your serious self to the office as soon as possible. Weaver won't be in a laughing mood."

"For sure!" Blaine agreed. "I'll see you there."

Jack hung up and grabbed the phone book. He opened it and fumbled his finger through the various numbers. Once targeted, he yanked up the receiver, punched the digits and waited.

"Good morning, the Washington Tribune," a woman's voice echoed. "How may I assist you?"

"Yes, good morning. I'd like to be connected to the desk of one Simone Wellington, please."

"Who may I say is calling?"

"Tell her it's Special Agent Jack Stanwick with the Federal Bureau of Investigation."

"The FBI..." Her tone rose. "Please hold, sir. I'll see if she is in."

"Thanks."

There's nothing better than an agent of the government calling on a Monday morning to get the week off and running. Jack enjoyed using his profession to get what he wanted. People stood at attention.

"Mr. Stanwick, she will be with you in a moment."

"Thanks."

Jack shook his head at Simone's headline then thumbed through a few of the pages. He stopped midway and saw an article about the shooting death of a young African-American boy from the projects.

Why isn't that getting national attention? Apparently, the missing white son of a governor is far more important than the killing of a poverty-stricken kid.

He huffed. *Everything must be sensationalized or controversial with the media getting the last word. Either the life of a story landed on the front page or the death of one was relegated to a small area on page six...lower left corner. They get to choose!*

Jack leaned against the wall. *Where is this woman?*

He remained on hold for what seemed to be an eternity when a rather soothing voice came upon his ear.

"Hello, this is Simone Wellington. May I help you?"

"Yeah...I mean, yes...you finally may." Jack squeezed the headline in his hand. "You wrote a story that appeared in the Washington Tribune. I'd like to know how you got your hands on the information."

"I'm sorry, who am I speaking with?"

He didn't like her. "I'm Special Agent Jack Stanwick with the Federal Bureau of Investigation."

"So you're an FBI man."

"Yeah, that's pretty much what I just said."

"Well, Mr. Stanwick, exactly what story are you referring to? I've written so many."

Jack knew this oversized attitude. He'd dealt with them before.

"The story you wrote regarding the missing son of Governor Woodbine from Virginia." Anger fluctuated in his tone.

"Oh, that story," Simone uttered. "You know Mr. Stanwick, I can't reveal my sources. It wouldn't be..." She paused. "How should I put this—ethical—on my part, now would it?"

Jack paced around the table. "Miss Wellington..."

"Please, call me Ms."

"Excuse me, Ms. Wellington. How do I put this delicately?" Jack knew with his job, he'd get more flies with honey than with vinegar. He altered his tone. "I'm working on a case which requires the utmost discretion. With that being said, I feel that today's headline could've hindered or even jeopardized my ongoing investigation."

"Mr. Stanwick, I'm a journalist, and with that being said, it's my job to report any newsworthy event to the public. I need to keep them informed of all the day's activities, not to mention those that unfold overnight. I'm not in a position to concern myself with every article coming over my desk, including those that disturb, disrupt, damage or even destroy cases for the

Federal Bureau of Investigation. Obviously, someone wanted this story to be in print or they wouldn't have leaked it to me."

He liked her even less. "I understand your position, Ms. Wellington, but do you know the position I'm now in?"

"Pertaining to what, Mr. Stanwick?"

"To the Governor's son, Ms. Wellington."

"Could you be more specific?"

"The first twenty-four hours are extremely crucial in discovering Carlton Woodbine's whereabouts."

"Of course, I know that. I've written articles on the very subject."

"Have you written about the many crackpots of our fair city who'll be calling the Bureau with bogus details?"

"No, I haven't."

"Well, it's time for a crash course."

She puffed. "I don't need..."

"First, we have the pranksters who're completely bored with their lives and need some excitement," he reported. "We also have the mentally-challenged who actually believe what their minds have created. Next are those saying he's at their location committing a crime; after all, he is missing and therefore must've done something bad and is on the lam. Then last, but certainly not least, are the ones convinced they've captured Carlton. Usually he's locked in a closet, cupboard or even the dryer. How do they know it's him, you might ask? His picture is in the paper, and of course it's followed up with 'is there a reward'?"

"I didn't..."

"Wait! I've got to give you examples, just in case you want to make it fodder in your next expose."

"There is no need..."

"You see Ms. Wellington, one call will come from a hysterical woman screaming that Carlton is hiding inside a potato bin at her aunt's house, or he'll be up in another woman's attic attempting to steal a wedding gown her great grandmother wore during the Civil War. Better yet, he's been locked in the closet by a man with a kitchen knife holding him at bay..."

"Are you quite finished?"

"And miss out on the best one?" Jack smirked. "No, I couldn't do that to you." He put his foot on the kitchen chair and leaned in. "What about the man who called to say that his four-year-old daughter's tricycle was stolen and the thief happened to be the spitting image of the picture from your newspaper, you know, the one showing Carlton in a three-piece suit shaking hands with the President of the United States? I figured he must've needed a ride home from the gala and the little girl's three-wheeler was his only choice. No wonder nobody can find him. He's still pedaling to his house."

"Mr. Stanwick..."

"Ms. Wellington, I'm not done. I've got one more thing to say." He wasn't ready to let his anger go. "I wanted you to know, in case you haven't written any articles about it, how the agents would and should feel about your success. Most, who're working on their own serious cases, will be reassigned. Their new jobs will be to man the phones, write down unnecessary drivel and deal with the barking commands of an anxious Director. You see, one never knows when a piece of crucial evidence might or might not happen from the hundreds to thousands of calls they'll receive over the coming days. Let me just say, the overflow of joy and contentment will be abundant. After all is said and done, who doesn't love talking to cranks, oddballs, screwballs or your run-of-the-mill nut jobs? I would be extremely grateful, and they should be too, just in case you didn't know." He breathed out. "Now I'm finished."

There was a pause. "Mr. Stanwick, just in case you didn't know, I now know. Point taken!"

"Oh, I didn't know I was making one."

"I've obviously created a problem, so now I'll fix it," she claimed. "First I need to put you on hold for a moment or two."

She's probably looking me up on the Internet or phoning her sources for a complete dossier on me.

He picked up his coffee and paced while sipping.

What's taking her so long?

He kept pacing.

She must've done this as a joke, the nasty...

"Mr. Stanwick, I'm sorry that took so long. I had to make sure that you were you."

"Well, I am me."

"I know, so what do you need from me?"

"What do I need?" His shoulders straightened.

That was too easy.

He smirked. "I need you to hold off from printing anything more about Carlton Woodbine. I mean, just for now."

"Sure, why not? It's only the hottest story on the planet," she bellowed. "I know, I'll just quit my first great job and go on a second-rate vacation to a third-world country. Problem solved!"

Jack jerked his foot off the chair and slammed it on the floor. "I didn't say that."

"I didn't think so."

Jack grunted and yanked the phone away from his mouth. He jerked around, plopped his butt against the edge of the table and shook his head. He edged up his hand. "I take it that's out of the question."

"How could you ask me that? I mean, that's what I live for."

36

"I know I asked for too much, I get that," he pleaded. "I just…" His breath expired. "I just wanted to ask some questions. Maybe get some answers to go on."

There was a moment of silence. "You may ask me another question. Just this time, don't hit so close to home."

A smile beamed forth as Jack lifted from the table. "And I promise, it won't conflict with your ethical conscience."

"It better not, Mr. Stanwick."

He heard a hint of laughter so he chuckled. "By the way, you can call me Jack."

"Fine, and you may call me Simone."

"Was it a man or a woman who contacted you?"

"It was a man."

Jack felt more at ease.

"Did the source give you his name?"

"No, he didn't."

"How did he know it was the governor's son?"

"My source gave me a positive identification of Carlton Woodbine," she replied. "The color of his hair and eyes, height and weight; you know, his physical features. He even described what Carlton was wearing the night he was abducted…"

"But he could've been recounting a stock photo of Carlton that was issued somewhere," Jack asserted. "I swear, that kid's in the paper weekly for his shenanigans."

"If you hadn't interrupted me, I would have told you what sealed the deal for me."

"I'm sorry, my mind is always one step behind my mouth."

"What I was about to say was Chevron Reynolds, a.k.a. 'Gossip Guy', writes a column for the paper. He frequently drops by my desk to shoot the breeze. Basically, I get the dirt before it comes out in the morning edition. Most days, he's bursting at the seams to tell somebody before it hits the street, and that someone is always me..."

"Is he your source?"

"No, and stop busting in on my story."

"I'll stop, but are you closer to the end than the beginning?"

"You'll just have to find that out when I'm finished."

Shoot! He dropped down into the kitchen chair.

"As I was saying, I'm his go-to girl, and he let loose about the night Carlton and his girlfriend, Amanda, got into their huge fight. "I'll spare you all of that."

"I appreciate that."

"Anyhow, I asked if he had pictures of it, and of course, Chevron prances away to get them. When I saw the various photographs, I took note of what they both were wearing. It's nice to see what the rich can afford. I'm a clotheshorse myself."

"A what?"

"Never mind!" she stated. "Anyways, Chevron's photos are not printed in our paper. Mostly there for his amusement. And if anybody knows the comings and goings of the rich and infamous in Washington, DC, it's the 'Gossip Guy'."

Jack stared at the ceiling. "And what does all this mean to my case?"

"Chevron told me the wealthy would never be caught dead wearing the same outfit twice, let alone being photographed in them. One could be shunned by the upper echelon and that is high society suicide. So now you can see what I mean."

"No, right now, I'm as blind as a bat."

"Jack, my source couldn't be recounting a stock photo since Chevron just took them. He has yet to upload them onto his blog."

"So, the only other person who would've known what clothes he had on is the kidnapper."

"That's what I was saying all along!" Simone exhaled. "I guess you have to be a journalist to understand what I was talking about."

"You're probably right." *Wrong! Just tell me straight out instead of giving me useless details.* "Did you probe further?"

"Of course! I felt he knew something and was not letting on, or maybe wanted money for the story, so I asked him some leading questions. He started to hem and haw and seemed to be in an awful hurry to get off the phone. I stopped and went with a different approach. First I thanked him for his information and stated how much it would help my career..."

It's all about positive reinforcement."

"Yes, and the reason I know so much about the subject is I'd done an article about it a couple of years back when I interviewed the world-renowned psychiatrist Millicent Sentinel. She spoke of mood modification. My editor loved the concept so much that instead of doing a small section on her it ended up being a grand expose with photographs."

Jack reigned her in. "What happened with your source?"

"After that, he seemed to relax. I politely asked his name, but there was hesitation so I eased up and asked how he knew about Carlton Woodbine. He answered with 'I just do'.' I followed another train of thought. I told him that anything he could tell me would bring my article alive."

"Good idea."

"The main thing was it worked. He slowly started telling me something about a place somewhere in Virginia. Supposedly, it was late at night when they both had met. I asked for what purpose? Again, he clammed up. I'm thinking to myself, why tell me any of this if you're not going to tell me any of this? I thanked him for the information he gave me, but unfortunately, it wasn't enough to warrant a story."

"Then what happened?"

"Out of nowhere, he began to open up. I couldn't get a word in edgewise so I just wrote as fast as my fingers could. This guy prattled on and on. It was delightful, until the fool abruptly stopped in mid-sentence and hung up on me. I was livid! There was so much more to ask."

"Yeah, whether he was a nut job or not."

"It had crossed my mind, but something in his voice seemed genuine. I could sense it. Call it my journalistic hunch."

"You've got to rely on your gut."

"There's more," she stated. "While I felt what he said was sincere, at the same time something inside me wasn't settling right."

"What do you mean?"

"It was an eerie sensation, like I've talked to this man before or knew him somehow. I just can't place it."

"Maybe it's a premonition."

"More like déjà vu."

Jack sat up in the chair. "This place you were told about, did he happen to mention a name?"

"When he said it, I imagined a charming stone cottage, you know, the picturesque kind with a flowing creek and a paddlewheel for electricity."

"Yeah, I know."

"It's called painting you a picture. Oh, forget about it. The name is Granite's Mill."

Jack's mouth fell wide open. "Really?"

"Yes."

"Did you get an exact location?"

"I might have, but I'd have to look at my notes."

"Good, see if there's anything else, possibly something you're not thinking of."

"What's this all about?"

Jack ditched the question. No more information should flow. "I just wanted to know." His mind fought for a thought. "It's good record-keeping."

"I'll get them."

A desk drawer opened.

"They're here somewhere…"

He could hear the effort in her voice.

"Ok, I found them. Let me see, I'm skimming. It appears I've written down a lot." She paused. "I said to the man that he could've gathered all of this information from the press. The man remarked he had a tidbit that nobody else knew unless they were there." She stopped. "I forgot about this. It's a good thing I keep great notes."

"What is it?" Jack yelped. "What did he say?"

"He said that Carlton had a tattoo of the family crest on his upper right shoulder blade and that it had the colors of blue and yellow with some red," she replied. "It also had two scrolls. The one above read, 'The Ancient Arms of,' and the one below it read, 'Woodbine.'"

Jack gasped.

"I went back and took another look at our stock photos on the computer to see if we had any of him shirtless."

"Did you find any?"

"No, and there's nothing written about him getting a tattoo. I don't know how I could have forgotten that item. My memory is usually spot-on."

"Speaking of spot, did you write down the name of the town?"

"I'm skimming again." Simone paused once more. "Found it. The name is Rockfort."

Jack jumped up. *Yeah!* He punched his fist into the air. "I need to ask you a huge favor."

"What?"

"I need to be informed of any more leaks you receive regarding this particular story. It's very important. Take down my cell number. You can call me day or night."

She puffed. "This case must be of extreme importance if an agent of the FBI is questioning me about a story I just ran this morning."

"It is."

A drawer slammed and was followed by the shuffling of papers.

Jack understood her mood.

"Simone, listen to me. If you print anything about this it could imperil my whole case, if it hasn't already." His voice grew more urgent. "I need you. Please, help me."

"Fine," she blurted out. "I'll do this really huge favor for you, but there's one condition."

He nearly shouted. "Name it."

"When this case is solved, I get the exclusive story from you, a very intimate interview. I want full disclosure of all information pertaining to this case, every detail, no matter what it is." She paused. "Deal?"

Jack paced the floor. "Deal!" He exhaled. "But I need your full cooperation."

"You've got it."

"Thanks, I really appreciate it."

"I want you to know that I'm putting part of my career on the back burner in choosing this alliance."

"I want you to know that I'm putting my butt on all four of them in choosing this alliance."

"Is that all, Jack?"

He leaned against the wall. "No."

"What're you taking next?"

"Any and all information your source tells you, no matter how trivial. I need to be notified immediately when he calls. Is that clear?"

"Yes, sir!" she declared in what Jack thought was a military tone.

"At ease, Simone."

"Goodbye, Mr. Stanwick, and don't forget to honor our commitment."

"I'll honor it." He heard a dial tone. *And a goodbye to you too!*

He slammed down the receiver and dropped his head. After taking some deep breaths, Jack lifted the phone and dialed the Bureau. He walked over to the cupboard and grabbed out a granola bar. With the wrapper ripped away, a huge bite took a chunk off.

"Federal..."

"Good you're at the office."

"Is your mouth full?" Blaine asked. "I can barely understand you."

"Yeah, I'm chomping on my breakfast."

"Yuck! You and those granola bars."

"Listen, I called that reporter, Simone Wellington, at the Washington Tribune and coaxed her into supplying me with the information she got, and will keep giving me from her source. The thing is I forgot to give her my cell number. She'll soon realize it and call me at the Bureau. Just one problem. I'm not there."

"This is true, but I'll give it to her."

"Good. I need all the clues I can get."

"Speaking of clues, what'd she tell you? Give me the skinny."

"She was given the information from a male source that telephoned her." Jack strived to sell his version of the events. "I gave her a sob story about ruining my case and she couldn't have been sorrier. She told me everything, which justified my gut instincts. The body found at Granite's Mill is most likely the governor's son, and that's not even the best part. Her source stated that Carlton Woodbine had a tattoo on the back of his right shoulder. I remember seeing something there, but due to the bloating it was hard to get a reading on it. Still, I felt it was something."

"Pay dirt!"

"Tell me about it. I'm just glad she folded."

"Way to go," Blaine hailed. "You're the man."

"I am the man," Jack uttered, confident his partner bought into his tale.

"Now you just have to locate her source."

"Easier said than done."

"You'll find him. Remember, you're the man."

44

"Yeah...." Jack lowered his tone. "I'm the man."

"Don't sound so licked. You've got Simone Wellington on your side."

"She's on my side." *Is it my good or bad side is the question?*

"Have you looked her up on any of the databases?"

"No, but I've got a sneaking suspicion she was surfing the World Wide Web during our little chat."

"She had to look you up to make sure you were the real McCoy..."

"It's just that I heard many a keystroke going down, and my gut's telling me that my name's on every one of them."

"Gathering information is sort of her specialty."

"Speaking of information, Edgar should have the identity of our John—or should I say—Jane Doe," Jack remarked. "I'm getting in the shower then going over to see him. Do me a favor. If Simone Wellington calls the Bureau looking for me, would you..."

"I know...give her your cell number."

"Well, I'm glad somebody is working hard on this case."

"Just be glad it's me."

"Touché. You got this round. Next one's on me."

"We'll see," Blaine said. "Au revoir."

Jack chuckled. "Auf Wiedersehen."

Chapter 4

Upset that the chemical hadn't yet been perfected, Buford brooded into Prescott Chemicals. He lurked past the receptionist, skulked up to Henry's door and gave it a knock.

"It's unlocked."

Buford turned the knob and sulked in. "You wanted to see me."

Henry was on the computer and paid him no mind.

"I picked up the Washington Tribune on my way here."

"Listen, I need to speak to you about the formula you're working on." His eyes still on the computer.

Buford tossed the newspaper on the desk. "But first, I think you need to look at the front page. A reporter by the name of Simone Wellington wrote an interesting article."

"Not now. I'm too busy looking at some specs."

Buford knew that mood. "Please, just look at it." He remained a little on edge.

"What now?" Henry grabbed the newspaper and opened it.

Buford pointed. "I saw this."

"Yeah, so the governor's son is missing. Who gives a damn? Why're you showing me this?" He threw it into the trashcan by his desk.

Buford despised his boss more times than not. Henry could be a real jerk. "You need to read this." He bent over, picked it out and laid it back in front of him.

"Argh! For heaven's sakes, I'll do it later."

"No, read it right now."

"Look, I said later!" Henry yelled. "At the moment, I need to speak to you about the formula."

"Read it!"

"Who're you giving commands to?"

"Sorry." Buford backed off. "Please, just look at it."

Henry glared at him with gritted teeth. "It better be worth my time."

"Trust me. It'll be worth it."

Henry lifted the paper. His eyes moved from side to side. When finished, his scowl resumed. "Why'd you want me to read this?"

Buford wrung his hands together. "Remember that kid we grabbed off the street in Richmond."

"What about him?"

"Um..." He felt shaky. "At the time he looked awful familiar to me."

"What do you mean—familiar?"

A lump settled in Buford's throat. "That kid; he looked like somebody I'd seen before."

"I got that," Henry croaked. "Stop beating around the bush."

Buford inhaled. "It finally dawned on me who he is or was."

"What do you mean—was?" Henry stood up from his chair. "What the hell are you telling me?

"Um...I'm telling you, ah..." Buford twitched. "I think it was the governor's son."

"You think..." Henry's face became distorted. "You better know! Don't come waltzing in here and say something you know nothing about."

"I know..." Buford cowered with a lowered head. His stomach burned. "I know it was him." He cringed and waited for the verbal assault.

"Oh, now you know!" Henry howled. "That's damn good to know." He put his hands on his head. "Do you realize that the FBI will be all over this thing? What're we going to do?" His fists bashed on the desk.

Buford jumped back as his body trembled.

"Damn it! Of all the people to grab." Henry yanked at his necktie to loosen it. "I cannot believe this!" His hands were shaking as he brought them back to his head. "How long before you get that damn formula perfected?"

Buford didn't want to make him any angrier. Henry was a very violent man. The outbursts were legendary and burnt into his psyche. "Please, calm down. I've got it under control."

"Under control!" Henry leaped out of his chair, dashed around the desk and lunged at Buford. He grabbed him by the front of his shirt and lifted his slight body off the floor. "You've got nothing under control. The formula's a mess. Bodies are scattered over two states and you're telling me to calm down!" His face was wrenched with anger as the spit flew from his lips. "Do you know that we're the only chemical plant within a few hundred miles of this frigging debacle? We're the only one in the region capable of producing these chemicals. It's only a matter of time before the FBI starts snooping around our backyard." He tightened his grip. "You're a complete screw-up!"

"I know! I know!" Buford grasped the hardened hands. "Please, let go..." He tried to shake loose. "You're hurting me!"

Henry hurled him to the ground.

48

Buford flew into a couple of chairs and knocked them over with a crashing thud. He rolled over and clutched his side. "Oh, my back." His body convulsed. "I'm in such pain."

"You should be, fool," Henry lifted his leg. "I should kick some damn sense into that thick head of yours."

Hearing that tirade, Buford hunched. "No."

Henry slammed his foot down on the floor. "Get up!"

Buford climbed to his knees, gained his footing and looked forward. At first sight, double-vision appeared. He stood for a second, allowing his eyes to find their focus. After wobbling to the wall, he grasped his back and rubbed it. "You didn't need to do that." His eyes welled up. "I'm doing the best I can."

Henry yanked open a drawer and pulled out a bottle of Jack Daniel's. He leaned against the desk, poured some, brought the glass to his quaking lips and belted it back. He filled it again, sat down in his leather swivel chair and lounged back. "What I need you to do now is go to the lab and check on the progress of TB4711 and report to me about any further developments." He took another swig of his drink. "And there better be developments."

"Go to hell!"

"I'm already there." Henry sat forward. "Now move it!"

Buford turned around without a word and snatched the brass handle to secure himself. He swung open the sturdy oak, stepped out and slammed it shut.

"Damn it!" Henry rummaged through his Rolodex, picked up the phone and punched its various numbers. While waiting, he poured another drink. After filling it to the brim, he lifted the tumbler with his shaking hand, put it to his lips and slung it back.

"Hello, Speaker of the..."

"Logan, its Henry Prescott."

"Why're you calling here? You know never to use this phone."

"I forgot my briefcase at the house. My damn cell phone is in it along with your cell phone number."

"Why'd you call?"

"I'm in a panic and I need to talk to you."

"It better be good if you're calling me on the office phone," Logan snarled.

"Oh, it's a doozy."

"Then I will call you back on my cell phone."

Henry hung up and poured himself another drink. His private line rang. "Hello."

"What's so important that you had to interrupt my day?"

"I need to..." His voice lowered. "I need to ask you..."

"Speak up, I can't hear you."

"I need to ask if you..." Henry cleared his throat.

"Will you spit it out? I'm a busy man."

"Have you seen today's edition of the Washington Tribune?"

"No, I haven't."

"Damn!"

"Why, what's the big deal?"

Henry tossed back his drink and gulped it down. "The deal is you always read it. It's like an obsession with you."

"I've been in congressional meetings all morning," Logan snapped. "I am the Speaker of the House. I pretty much have to attend those sorts of things."

Henry glowered. "Well, you need to read it."

"Why?

"Because the Governor of Virginia's son has disappeared and there's an article about it on the front page."

"And I need to know that because?"

"Logan, do what you want. Read it. Don't read it. I don't give a rat's ass."

"What's the big deal? I could care less about some measly governor's son, so why read it?"

Henry emptied the rest of the bottle into his tumbler. "Then I guess this conversation is over."

"Wait!"

"What?"

Logan exhaled. "I didn't mean to..." He stopped. "It's just been one of those days."

"I'm having one of them myself." Henry lifted his drink. "Thank God I've got another bottle of JD."

"You've been drinking?"

"You'll soon be too."

"Ok, what's going on? Talk to me."

Henry huffed. "I've been trying to do just that."

"Well, now I'm all ears."

Henry was leery about telling him the news. He knew Logan's reaction would be stinging. "When, or if you read the Washington Tribune, you'll see an article about the Governor of Virginia's son."

"You've said that already. The kid's missing. I got that. Why do you care? Better yet, why should I care?"

"Oh, you'll care..."

"Look, I'm the Speaker of the House, two positions away from the Presidency of the United States of America. Why on earth should I be concerned with such a trivial matter? That's what the FBI is for. Their agents will take care of it so don't worry about such nonsense."

Henry despised Logan's pompous attitude. Everything was always about him. "Buford was just in my office and told me that the last guy who was grabbed off the street and injected—you know, the drunken one I told you about—well, he's the Governor of Virginia's missing son."

"What?" The outburst was deafening.

"Wait, it gets better."

"How does it get better?"

"He's dead."

"Oh, my God," Logan shouted. "What the..."

"For now, you need to calm down."

"Calm down! Is that what you just said? Calm down?"

"Logan..."

"How could this have happened?" The receiver rattled. "How?"

"I don't know, but you need to quiet down. People will hear you."

"Screw them! They always hear me yelling at some imbecile. I have to. It's part of my job description."

Henry clutched another bottle of JD and unscrewed the cap.

"Damn it! Are you sure about Buford? He could've made a mistake. You know what a moron he is. He doesn't get anything right. Look at the formula for instance."

"I don't think this a mistake." Henry filled the entire tumbler. "Buford's an idiot, but I don't think he would come to me with this kind of news if it weren't correct. I was so mad that I grabbed his shirt and threw him to the floor."

"You need to get that temper of yours under control."

"Me?" Henry bellowed. "Your temper is worse. Not to mention the haughty attitude that comes with it."

"Enough already!"

"Yeah, this is going nowhere." Henry downed his drink. "We need to calm down and think this through."

"I know."

"Besides Buford, who else was on that mission?"

"Just Arvin Horton and Harvey Welch."

"Do the other members of M.A.G.O.C. know about this?"

"Doubt it. I just found out about it myself."

"There are going to be severe ramifications over this fall out," Logan announced. "Our mission, everything we've worked for, could ultimately be compromised. I'll have to pull some serious strings behind the scene to keep abreast of any findings. In the meantime, they've got to be extra careful moving forward. No more mistakes can take place. You got that? I'm counting on you to pull this off. When this happens, and trust me, it will. The benefits are going to be astronomical."

"Yeah, I know."

"Just remember the bargain I made with you."

"I always do."

"Our goals are top notch, as long as those two stupid morons don't screw things up."

"I wouldn't let them hear you say that."

"What're Buford and Arvin going to do? Inject me? Lest you forget who's running this show."

"Don't you forget, they're all you've got," Henry croaked. "I wouldn't get them in an uproar."

"You know me, I'd never say it to their face." Logan laughed. "I'm a bureaucrat. I don't get dirt on me. That's why I leave the heavy lifting to you."

"Well, I can only lift so far."

"Your point being?"

"I can only carry orders so far and after that, they've got to pull their own weight."

"With you ordering, they'll keep pulling."

"Yeah, but they need to know that since you're the primary beneficiary, you're in their corner. They're counting on you to keep your promises."

"And I will. Besides, to their knowledge, the money is in an off-shore account that I buried so deep in paperwork not even the FBI, the CIA and Scotland Yard combined could find it. There's no need for them to worry."

"Easy for you to say. They're not coming to your chemical company," Henry growled. "I'm going to have agents crawling up my ass like flies invading some warm cow..."

"Shoot, you worry too much."

"I don't worry enough."

"I'll do everything within my power to deflect the investigation," Logan stated. "We've got brothers in various locations, especially in the ranks of the FBI and the CIA, for that matter. We'll have to get word to Arvin about getting just those members together for a meeting. They won't be told anything about our plan. The only thing they're for is to keep me abreast about the investigation. That'll begin our intervention."

"I'll call him."

"Why don't we get together tonight at your plant for a small meeting to set things in motion?" Logan suggested. "It'll be me, you and Arvin."

"Don't forget about Buford?"

"Oh, yes. Can't forget the mad scientist. How about 10:00pm?"

"That should work."

"By the way, what exactly happened the night the Governor's son was injected? I need to know so I'm on top of things."

"Well, as Buford told to me..."

"Again, I'm questioning that source."

Henry continued, "I guess they saw this guy staggering down the street, and by their calculations, he was obviously drunk. An easy mark. They figured he wouldn't put up much of a struggle like the other two had, especially the security guard. He landed a few punches before they took him down."

"So did Harvey's hard head." Login laughed. "The backstabbing bastard got what he deserved from Arvin."

"Still, he didn't need to die. A good working over would've shut his mouth."

Logan sneered. "I told the idiot to do just that, but you know what a bulldog he is. I don't know why we brought on an ex-boxer who has had too many brain cells beaten out of him."

"Arvin is the muscle behind this operation. He was the one who asked the kid if he needed a ride somewhere. The young man climbed right into the van and gave his address then laid his head on the seat and fell asleep. They drove to a dark side street and Buford injected him."

"Then what happened?"

"The guy woke up when the metamorphosis began. Unfortunately, sometime during the process he died just like the other two. The thing is, Buford said this kid reacted differently. He didn't change as rapidly. As a matter of fact, it took a lot longer. That suggested the formula is getting better and pretty close to near ready. It just needs a little more tweaking."

"Good. Where's he storing it?"

"He's using the small vat in the basement that I had installed. The elixir was poured in and other chemicals were added so it would retain complete stability."

"Why in a vat?" Logan asked. "Isn't that overdoing it?"

"Not at all!" Henry placed his feet on the desk. "The formula was extremely potent. It changed a boy into a girl in a few seconds. This kid was about a hundred and twenty pounds soaking wet. Do you know how much had to be added to buffer the original solution? Buford calculated everything to attain what we've got. Everything has to be exact. That's why he's having issues getting it perfected. Besides, the vat's only six feet by nine feet, and the solution is only a few feet deep. I had a spigot installed so he could test as often as needed. The containment unit is hooked up to a computer and some other items. Let's just say it cost me a small fortune. Plus, nobody gets suspicious if it looks like we're making something new, and nobody goes down there without my approval either."

"I might know someone who can help Buford perfect the formulation."

"You want to bring another person in on this chaos?" Henry dropped his feet to the ground. "Too many cooks will spoil the broth."

"This chef is a physicist."

Henry knew Logan's mind was always scheming. "Who is it?"

"A couple of weeks ago, I met a French physicist at a fundraiser for the Green Initiative Bill. It was held in Miami at the Hollingsworth Hotel. This woman was the keynote speaker and gave a lecture about nuclear fusion and its effect on the environment. She was touting how beneficial this energy was over its alternatives and was lambasting natural gas while putting another nail into the hydro-fracking coffin. I couldn't believe it. I've got major money invested in solar and wind and their stocks have been rising up ever since. However, my oil and natural gas have plummeted somewhat on the market, but I digress."

It's about time!

"So after the presentation, I found out her name and where she's from. This woman also travels from city to city lecturing at various venues. She speaks at numerous universities across the states filling our young minds with her good news. One piece of good news is she's quite exquisite."

I'm sure.

"Another piece is Congress finally listened to her and the other speakers. After creating a bill, it went straight to the senate floor for a vote."

"I heard the President signed it into law last week."

"You heard right."

"I bet you almost had a heart attack!" Henry jested. "You've only been bitching about it for the last few months."

"I barely recovered, but now I'm seeing this woman, and she saved me from the coronary's clutches."

"Again, is there a point to all of this?"

"Yes, I'm getting to it."

"Well, get to it quicker. I've got a company to run, and a Buford to control."

"Remember, you called me for advice. You'll have to listen to it now."

Henry puffed. "Go ahead."

"As I was saying, I asked this delightful creature what her name was even though I knew it. She said it was Lydia Reome. I gave her mine then asked her to dance. I was floored when she agreed, so off to the dance floor we went. What a beauty she is; petite with a succulent shape and has a powerhouse of intelligence. You could talk to her all night about any subject, but that wasn't really on my radar, if you get my drift..."

"Oh, I got it," Henry blurted out. "Just get to the gist without—drifting."

"During the course of the evening, and a couple bottles of wine, we discussed our professions and whatever else came up, and lots of things came up."

"You're drifting."

Logan exhaled. "I eventually asked her to my room, and again she was in agreement. I couldn't wait to get her in my lair."

Henry grimaced. *Oh, God, shoot me right between the eyes.*

"When we finally got there, I ordered some champagne. We climbed onto my king-sized bed and talked while waiting for it to arrive. Within fifteen minutes room service was at my door with a bottle of Dom Perignon, and trust me, it was a very good year."

"Why are you telling me this? We're not college girls lying around the sorority house painting our toenails."

"Lighten up, will you?" Logan groused. "Where was I?"

"A very good year."

"Oh, yes. After we polished off the Dom things loosened dramatically, especially my tongue."

"Are you alluding to pillow talk?"

"Of course!"

"Then tell me the non-pillow talk, if you get my drift?"

"I get it," Logan retorted. "Lydia asked me, in a little girl's voice, to tell her a story. It was quite the turn-on, I might add."

"No adding either," Henry growled. "Just subtract the innuendos and tell me what counts."

"Well, the thing was I couldn't think of one. I mean, my mind went blank. At that point I decided to tell her a whopper, so M.A.G.O.C. came out."

"What did you just say?"

"Relax, Henry. I just told her about the organization, not our plot."

"I'm surprised."

"There's really no need to be. All I said was what the initials stood for—Men Against Government Overtaking Control— and how we're not going to let Big Brother take away our rights."

"How did she respond?"

"She gave me a weird look and asked me why I worked for the government if I felt so negatively about them. I told her that my employment afforded me an opportunity to keep tabs on their affairs, thus allowing me to inform my fellow members of all activities they're involved in. Remember the old adage by Machiavelli, 'Keep your friends close and your enemies closer'...you know, my modus operandi. She had never heard that analogy before and thought me to be charming. I was earning points at every turn."

"You're not concerned she might say something to someone about it? If the news got around about our activities and the government found out, you'd be fired instantly. Not to mention they'd probably water-board you for the whereabouts of other members. You can't trust the tongue of a woman."

"Well, I've got an insurance policy to make sure she doesn't talk."

"What is that?"

"My fair Lydia was a little blitzed that night and had her own loose lips." Logan sniggered. "She told me about her past and that's such a no-no. Apparently, she had an affair with this high-ranking official in the French government by the name of Pierre Montpelier. He's married to that French actress who won an Oscar for best actress in a foreign film a couple of years back. I can't think of her name off hand."

"You mean, Paulette Pomier?"

"Yes, that's her name. I forget you're an awards buff."

"It's just a hobby." Henry assured him. "Just continue with your sordid yarn."

"My Lydia told me that she met this fellow, Pierre, at a conference about alternative energy sources. Due to the crisis in the Middle East, which happens every other week, they wanted to rely less heavily on them for fuel."

"Smart thinking."

"Well, not so much on her part. She told me that they had this fantastic fling, fell in love and began dating. Supposedly, he was to leave his wife and marry her. How wrong she was? In fact, Paulette suspected and hired a private investigator to watch her husband's activities. Of course, the infidelity was discovered. The detective's photographs, which he took at several locations, showed some racy scenes which became public in various newspapers and on the Internet. The wife hit the roof. Both of them were severely chastised and Lydia was forced to resign from her lucrative career as a professor at a prestigious university. Evidently, she became the fall girl with news organizations portraying her as a home- wrecker. Paulette milked the situation while Lydia was asked to leave the country, at least until the story subsided. She told it all."

"What if she goes back to France?"

"I don't think that will happen soon," Logan retorted. "Lydia's livid and very bitter over the whole incident. She said that the French government gave her beau a slap on the hand, but she was cast to the media wolves. Her life was turned upside-down. The press pulled no punches and hauled out every lover she had. When they used her up, she was asked to make herself scarce. She is a woman scorned and wants revenge."

"I don't think we should get mixed up with this unstable girl."

"Nonsense, Lydia could help us with our problem. She's a top-notch physicist. Chemicals are in her background. You can see why I told her about M.A.G.O.C. She could help us with our problem and we in turn can help with hers. We'll team her up with Buford to perfect TB4711, our formula for the future."

"What if she talks?"

"Lydia will say nothing or I'll drudge it up all over again," Logan avowed. "I'll let the media know exactly who she is. Nobody will go to her lectures. Moms will boycott the universities she will be booked at. Not to mention the conservative Christian right will chase her with proverbial pitchforks and torches while quoting bible scriptures they barely live by. She'll have to seek asylum in some remote country."

"Remind me never to cross you."

"You're my friend. I'd never do anything dastardly to you."

Yeah, right. Henry didn't trust Logan. "How're we helping this girl?"

"I've got some ideas roaming around in my head."

"You always do."

"In my profession, I have to."

"I'm not sure about this."

"Why?" Logan groaned. "Do you want to wait weeks, possibly months for Buford to get the formula perfected? He's leaving a slew of dead bodies that will connect to your chemical company. The FBI is already looking for the scapegoat. Do you want to be on death row?"

"Of course not!"

"Me either."

Henry considered what Logan peddled.

"Neither of us would survive that ordeal."

"What should we do? It's your ballgame."

"We've got to do this as a team."

"What makes you think she'll give up her lecture circuit?" Henry uttered. "I mean, is this proposal even feasible?"

"Listen to me. Lydia's coming to spend some time with me after her lecture tomorrow at Princeton. She told me it's tiring traveling from city to city and staying in one hotel after another, living out of her suitcase. She's prime for a new beginning. We'll offer her a position in your laboratory at the chemical plant. Tell her you're working on a top-secret formula and you need someone of her skill set to help with it. She might accept."

"What if she doesn't?"

"Lydia has to be employed to keep her work visa current. Otherwise, she'll have to leave the United States."

Henry rubbed the back of his neck.

"Look, she doesn't need to know what's happening at first. Ease her into it. Before long, she'll be up to her eyeballs in the whole charade. Anyhow, as I told you before, we hit it off beautifully. I feel Lydia is ready to settle down and establish roots somewhere so why not here in Washington, DC?"

"It seems to me she's going from one governmental affair into another."

"Let me worry about that," Logan declared. "You just worry about perfecting TB4711 so we can engage our plan soon. There are bills before the Senate, and if signed, they'll give Big Brother the needed leverage for gun control, later terms on abortions for the baby killers, more regulation on the tobacco companies that we have stocks in and higher taxes on the rich, which is you and me."

"I hear you."

"Well hear this. They're talking about taxing religion. That'll bring our beloved churches to the ground. There's also talk of legalizing illicit drugs to clear our massive deficit. Imagine the pandemonium. We've got corrupt lobbyists lurking everywhere, not to mention the left-wing liberals, our enemies, who're rattling their bureaucratic cages. It'll just be a matter of time before Congress will be installing cameras on every street corner. To hell with immigration. They want to know all the comings and goings of every citizen in America, and September 11th have given them just cause to trample on our First Amendment rights. The NSA is tapping phones left and right. The stampede will be unstoppable. You can now see the predicament. All of our predicaments."

Henry balked. "I hope you're right."

"You said it yourself, Buford's modifications are off. Lydia Reome might be our only hope in giving us the desired results. Contact our fellow brother, Arvin Horton. Run this by him. Also, don't forget to set up a meeting for tonight at your chemical plant around 10:00pm. We'll be able to discuss our future plans without those pesky flies on the wall. Oh, and by the way, Lydia's next speaking engagement is her last for a while. She might have to head back for France. You should really hire her for a consulting position. I'll bet you she takes it. Maybe the three of us can have drinks at the Back Alley Bar. I need a night out."

"It sounds good to me."

"I just hope that Buford cooperates with the idea."

"He has no choice," Henry bellowed. "Just leave him to me."

"Then it's a go?"

"I guess so."

"It needs to be so," Logan ordered. "Stop dragging your feet."

Henry breathed out. "Fine."

"From now on, call me on my cell phone. If I were you, I'd use my cell phone for all personal calls. I bought those burner phones and they're untraceable. So use them. You never know what the FBI, CIA or Homeland Security is up to. They love listening in on the public. That's how they get most of their cases closed."

"As usual, you're never wrong."

"You're right!" Logan crowed. "Goodbye."

Chapter 5

Agent Stanwick arrived at the J. Edgar Hoover Building and proceeded to the Medical Examiner's office. He entered the suite, gave it the once-over and observed that Edgar Cromwell was nowhere to be found. The place was just as he had last left it: well-arranged and tidy, but reeking of formaldehyde and death.

Jack wanted to read the coroner's results, and Lord knows he had seen enough of them, so he ambitiously poked around the desk to locate the reports on the three victims. Everything was orderly. He sifted through the papers and swiftly scanned each one in an attempt to secure the essential documents. Nearing the end of the pile, he heard a noise and immediately whipped his body around to witness what he thought was an apparition.

"Edgar!" Jack flinched, panicked at how frail the man had become since their last case. His face had become markedly drawn and he was hunched over to one side; he appeared extremely emaciated. Gaunt was ghostly upon him. A white lab coat, his trademark, floated along the floor as he tottered about the room. "How're you?"

"Busy, busy, busy," he replied. "I wish there were two of me."

"No. What I meant was, how do you feel?"

"As I always do," Edgar answered. "Vile."

Jack's forehead wrinkled. "Maybe you need some time off.

I mean, a long vacation can do a person a lot of good."

"There's never enough time..." Edgar growled. "Let alone for time off. I've so many cadavers to attend to. The fridge is teeming with them and I don't have the manpower to fulfill the access."

"Why don't you hire someone to assist you? That way you'd lighten some of your load."

"The government has a hiring freeze until they can steal the needed funds from another agency that desperately needs them," Edgar replied. "Not for nothing, I haven't had a raise in four years."

"How long have you been with the Bureau?"

"Since 1972, when I graduated from medical school. I was thirty."

Jack stood flabbergasted. Edgar looked a hundred and two. "Wow, that's a long time."

"It's taken up my whole life. For crying out loud, I'm married to it."

Jack wanted off this subject so he cleared his throat and redirected the conversation. "It's been mentioned that you have Carlton Woodbine's dental records. I hope they're not a match, especially during a reelection year."

"I just came from my lab. I wanted to double-check the results to be positive. I'm not going to mince words." A negative look fell over Edgar's face. "The dental records are a conclusive match to Carlton Woodbine."

"Damn it!" Jack threw his head to the side. "What am I going to tell his family?"

"I've even more disturbing news."

"What's that?"

"I stayed here late last night and performed Carlton's autopsy. Upon completion, I put a rush on all the findings and had them delivered here so I could give you the results this morning. Just follow me." Edgar shuffled ahead of him, exhibiting his wobbly gait as they entered the morgue. A light was flicked on and exposed a wall of refrigeration units. As he simultaneously opened two of them, a dry wave of cold air wafted by Jack's head. It was a stark reminder that death's assault could be summoned instantly. "Here are the bodies of Hal Bennett and Carter Reyes that came in over the weekend."

Jack gave them a cursory glimpse. Getting accustomed to the view always took him a second to shake off. He reached into his jacket pocket and retrieved his mini-recorder.

"You might want to also write this down," Edgar suggested. "Some instances will be quite procedural, especially when I discuss traumatic chemokinesis with you."

"Got it covered." Jack lifted a mini-recorder halfway out of his shirt pocket. "Plus, I always carry back-up." He whipped out a notepad and held tight to a pen. "You can imagine my embarrassment when my batteries went dead at an important meeting and I couldn't tell my partner, Blaine, about any of it because I was bored and daydreaming. Now, I have extra batteries in my glove compartment just in case."

"We've all been in that situation. "Well, now I'm ready."

"I want you to look at the wrists." Edgar spread out his unsteady hand.

Jack peered down and sealed the pictures into his mind. Having a photographic memory did have its benefits. "Got it."

Edgar moved his hand down further. "Now take a gander at the ankles."

His eyes seared another imprint into the brain. "What caused those marks?"

"I checked the impressions and found fibers on both, so I sent them off for examination. They arrived about forty minutes ago." He turned and took some papers off an upright tray and viewed them.

Jack flashed his eyes on Edgar's face. He waited to hear the verdict.

"My findings revealed that the two bodies recovered from Maryland were bound with textile rope. The kind used to tie together boxes or crates for shipping, and that's not all." He reached over and picked up another stack of reports. "I had further tests run on the fibrous material and discovered the chemical DMPT, which is the abbreviated form for Dimethylpatomalide. Do you want me to spell it?"

"No, I'll get a copy of your reports."

"Very well. Dimethylpatomalide is the main ingredient used in repellants to ward off insect infestation against such things as crop destruction. Also detected was Taflorlyzine, or TFLZ, which is a bonding agent so the insecticide will not only adhere to the crop, but will also cling to any insect that comes in contact with it to kill their larvae back at home. The third and final drug is Stametherol, or SMTR. It's a new preservative with a pungent odor to ward off any rodents that want to feast on a crop."

"Wow, those are some heady words!" Jack snickered. "The Food and Drug Administration sure has its work cut out for them."

Edgar nodded his head. "Yes, they do."

"How do you remember them and keep it all straight?"

"I've been doing this a long time. A very long time."

Jack grinned. *Yeah, since the dinosaurs' roamed.* He stepped back and dropped his expression. "Where do you think these chemicals came from?"

"If I had to take an educated guess, I'd say some type of chemical plant. One that's making pesticides and/or insecticides."

"I thought of that, especially when you said that word describing crop protection, Di...methyl...pat..." He rummaged through his notes.

"Dimethylpatomalide," Edgar pronounced. "It's a doozy."

"Yeah!" Jack chuckled. "Say that ten times fast."

"We'll just refer to it as DMPT."

"That I can handle."

Edgar grabbed something off the counter. "This is an electric magnifier." He switched it on and a beam of light appeared. "I want you to observe the carotid artery on the neck."

Jack peered in.

"Do you see this small amount of discoloration?"

He overlooked Edgar's flailing finger. "Yeah, it's a little bruise."

"That's an injection site."

"From a needle?"

"Yes, both of them were, and by the skin's reaction I'd say with something foreign. The area is raised and hard, and as you noticed quite bruised. The chemical or chemicals have caused a severe amount of irritation."

Jack threw on a pair of gloves and felt the abrasions on both necks.

"Now come here and inspect the third body." Edgar turned, teetered over to a stainless steel compartment and slid it open. "This is Carlton Woodbine. Look at the neck. He has the same raised and hard bruise on the carotid artery, but look at his wrists and ankles..."

Jack viewed them. "No marks."

"Exactly, no marks. Also of note, his blood alcohol level was 0.2 at the time of autopsy, but there was no alcohol in the blood of the other two victims."

Jack's eyes squinted. "Suggesting..."

"I'm suggesting that all three men were taken against their will. Think about it. Carlton was very inebriated at the time he was injected. According to their labs, the other two weren't, but both were restrained at the wrists and ankles when injected. They must have struggled violently to free themselves, thus sustaining the deep rope burns which explain the amount of fibers left in the wounds. Carlton could've easily been detained in his condition, especially if there was more than one individual holding him down. He was an easy target. Of course, I'm just speculating according to the evidence presented."

"As theories go, it's a sound one."

"Do you have any questions before we go into my office?"

"Did you see a tattoo on the back of Carlton's right shoulder?"

"I did."

"I couldn't make heads or tails of it." Jack shook his head. "Could you?"

"I employed a little trick I've picked up along the way," Edgar answered. "If you swab some hydrogen peroxide over a tattoo it tends to reveal itself."

"What was it?"

"A coat of arms with yellow and blue cresting and three red lions," Edgar replied. "I did some further digging and found that the Woodbine surname is of Scottish descent."

"How long ago did he have it done?"

"Quite recently; there was still a lot of scabbing."

Jack exhaled. "Could you get me a photo of it?"

"I've taken several," Edgar responded. "Come into my office. I have even better news for you." He skulked ahead and perched himself behind an ominous desk.

"Good, I could use some." Jack followed and sat down next to a bookshelf.

Edgar spread out his bony fingers, snatched up a pair of black horn-rimmed spectacles with thickset lenses and put them on.

He could probably see the International Space Station from here. Jack crossed his legs to mask his amusement.

"Here are the photos." Edgar handed them over.

Jack scanned them all. He grabbed one, he put it into his jacket pocket and tossed the rest back. "This will come in handy."

Edgar nodded. "Now if you think the things I told you back in the morgue were strange, we're now entering the realm of the bizarre." He picked up another envelope. "I've received the pathology and cytology reports from the autopsies I performed."

"What'd they say?" His pen poised to the pad of paper while his mini-recorder peeked out the front pocket of his blazer.

"I'm going to get a little technical on you so bear with me. I'll explain it all to you at the end."

"Good." Jack bobbed his head up and down.

"The pathology report renders the findings from the organ and tissue samples and the cytology report, the results of the blood and other body fluids."

"That wasn't bad." He then noticed Edgar's squalid grin.

Jack looked back down at his notepad.

"The reports concluded that each of the victims had some type of reflux due to foreign chemical compounds entering their bodies via an injection site. It caused the carotid arteries to become severely irritated. Due to this introduction, the cellular organelles have been altered. I've isolated five distinct chemical compounds that were throughout their lymphatic tissues, endocrine systems, nervous systems, interstitial tissue fluids and the dura mater of the brain."

Jack leaned over and wrote feverishly to keep up with the flow of information Edgar was firing out.

"Their chemistry screens, blood cultures, toxicity tests and complete blood counts were anarchic and their chromosomes had been displaced. There were also disorganized levels of estrogen, progesterone and testosterone. However, my most crucial finding was the pineal gland."

"A what?"

Edgar rose up from his chair and grabbed a medical encyclopedia. He brought it over to Jack, opened it and directed his doddering finger to the organ. "The pineal gland is found in the brain and is about the size of a pea. It's in this pocket near the splenium of the corpus callosum. The secretion from this gland starts the onset of puberty. The pineal glands in our victims were five times the normal size. Their magnitude is something I've never seen before. This gland produced an exceptional amount of excretion. I'd be given to say about ten times its subsequent production, which caused an extreme chemokinesis, thus producing a violent cytomorphoses."

Jack stopped, dropped his pen and leaned back in the chair. "Whoa, now that was bad."

"You spoke a little too soon earlier," Edgar quipped.

"I guess so."

"Now you know why I forewarned the need to break it down. I just wanted to heighten your medical knowledge."

"That you did!" Jack agreed. "I'd be given to say about ten times more than I've ever gotten before."

Edgar smirked.

"How about now giving me the elementary explanation?"

"In layman's terms, I said that the three victims were injected in the carotid artery. I showed it to you in the morgue."

"Yeah." Jack nodded.

"It caused a chemokinesis, which is the accelerated locomotion of cells due to the response of chemical stimuli. Basically, the cells in the bodies went berserk. They reacted against the foreign agent in a dramatic way, thus causing a cytomorphosis. It's an extreme metamorphosing of the body."

"So what you're saying is that the chemical compounds caused our guys to turn into she-males?"

"What I'm saying is once the chemical compounds were introduced into their bodies they initiated a metamorphosing affect, causing a male to female alteration, thus the appearance of both characteristics. Somewhere, in the process of morphing they died, not systematically bearing the exchange."

"But how? I mean, why? For what reason?" His fist tightened. "I've got so many darn questions."

"The how, I'm not quite sure. I can tell you one thing. I've never seen this before in all my years as a medical examiner," Edgar responded. "I once heard about this subject a long time ago when I was attending medical school. During an anatomy class, a Brazilian student told us about a tribe in South America who morphed their pubescent males into females for religious purposes. He swore on its authenticity. I felt the story was a fable, an old wives' tale."

"Wow," Jack muttered under his breath.

"As for the why, well, your knowledge of science is as good as my knowledge of the criminal...and the reason I'm sure is not to benefit society in any way, shape of form."

Jack leaned forward. "What about this guy, Harvey Welch?

How did he die?"

"A single strike put him down," Edgar replied. "There was blunt force trauma inflicted on the victim's skull. He never knew what hit him."

"Do you know how old he might be?"

"I'd say in his late fifties, but I could cut his leg in half and count the rings."

Jack chuckled. "No, I'll take your word for it." He enjoyed the momentary distraction.

"Now it's time to discuss the chemical compounds I found in the victims," Edgar said. "These are man-made, but I will refer to the four of them as synthetic."

"Four!"

"There is a fifth, but I will address that when we get to it."

Jack took a steady inhale. *Blaine, I'll trade places with you now!*

Edgar opened a folder. "The first chemical compound is Dycilatium. It was used throughout the 1950's for medicinal purposes and also to speed up the body's metabolic rate."

"Why, for what reason?"

"To have what was hyped as 'The California Contour.' In the late forties and early fifties, Hollywood had some of the most beautiful and shapely actresses governing the silver screen. Women wanted to look like Rita Hayworth, Jane Russell, Jayne Mansfield and Marilyn Monroe. The beauty industry was touted in many forms, with health being at the top of the list. The multivitamin craze was created. At that time, they were bulky and not easily absorbed so a pharmaceutical company created the aforementioned drug for better absorption. One particular side effect became very beneficial, an increase in the burning of fat cells. As I recall, when taken in pill form and accompanied by a healthy diet, it produced dramatic weight loss. Prescriptions flew off the shelves. It was also shown to reduce inflammation, and even some promising hormonal studies.

Women also talked of smoother, tighter and wrinkle-free skin with an added glow. It could've been revolutionary, but later research showed it had an increased risk of stroke. Plus it caused thyroid damage so the project was halted. The FDA discontinued all further production. To my knowledge no pharmaceutical companies make it anymore."

"Somebody's making it again."

Edgar nodded. "Do you need me to spell them for you? I know they're difficult. Some words are hard to pronounce."

"They must use every letter of the alphabet—twice." Jack twiddled the pen with his fingers. "I think I've got a handle on it. If I write it the way you say it, I'll be able to read it to another person. When we're done, I'll get a copy of everything so I'll know how to spell them the correct way."

"Good, then we'll proceed. The second chemical compound is Criamazine. It's a duel-functioning composite to normalize pH levels in a solution, thus keeping acidity and alkalinity at a steady seven while balancing hydrophilic and hydrophobic molecules. How are you doing?"

"Phew, I'll definitely need that one spelled out," Jack retorted.

"I already made a copy of everything, and gave an explanation of how it all works."

He respired with his mouth open. "You couldn't have said that at a better time."

"Now the third chemical compound is Triamerisol. It's a preservative that will keep the solution from going bad. The fourth chemical compound is Mandrolifid, and is used for stabilizing the amalgam so it won't dissipate. I mean, dry out." Edgar looked up. "Are you still with me?"

"Yeah, a little shaky, but so far so good," Jack responded. "Now the fifth and last compound is proving to be a challenge. It's what we call in the science world—a phytotoxin."

75

"A phytotoxin." Jack underlined the word.

"It's a toxin derived from an organic substance found in nature. An example of such is a plant. I've isolated three unique molecular structures, each being a phytotoxin. Somebody merged together the four synthetic compounds just spoke of to create a new fabrication. Do you understand what I'm saying?"

"I guess. I mean, I think so."

"The solution is made of three natural substances along with four synthetic compounds," Edgar remarked.

"So the four are keeping the fifth, which is really the three, from going amuck."

"Yes, but the natural components of the mixture might not last that long even with the synthetic compounds."

"Could you elaborate?"

"Let me see." Edgar tipped his head back. "Once removed from nature, phytotoxins can only be toxic for a short period of time. Our synthetic preservatives lack the key natural enzymes to cross-pollinate the organic structures. The simple sugar chain is very delicate and won't accept unnatural counterparts. Man hasn't come up with a low-cost natural preservative for them, as of yet. It's way too expensive. One can minimize the expense by using synthetic substances. Natural ingredients are a whole other ballgame. They have to be grown and harvested, which would cost triple or even quadruple the price. Nobody anywhere would pay those exorbitant prices. They'd be put out of business. There it is in a nutshell."

"So what you're saying is this stuff will lose its effectiveness, and soon?"

"That's what I've been alluding to. The premise is that once exposed to air, it'll lose potency. Even with the synthetic compounds, they can only keep it from degrading for a short time."

"Great." Jack smiled.

"The problem is science isn't a fixed strategy. It's ever changing. There are always exceptions to every rule."

"In other words..."

"This formulation, the organic part of it, wasn't discovered yesterday, recently, or even in the past couple of decades."

"How do you know that?"

"Since the sixties, when marijuana use skyrocketed, the government really cracked down on plants being brought into the United States from foreign countries, especially south of the border where it's commonly produced. Customs heavily scrutinizes all incoming agricultural and horticultural imports. Just the same, I don't think it entered via that route. It was most likely smuggled in, and I have another theory."

"What is that?"

"I feel it was brought in as a liquid suspension. If I were to guess, which is what I'm doing, I'd venture to say the probability of this solution being discovered some time ago isn't farfetched. Somehow it's been kept concealed, obviously stopping all deterioration which has allowed the potency. I'll bet the other ingredients were added long afterwards."

"How was it stored? I mean, if it was made so long ago."

"Well, there are many ways," Edgar replied. "Refrigeration and thermal cooling would suffice. We have the Peltier effect, which uses bismuth and tellurium thermal- coupling. Let me see, there's also silicon chip cooling through computers, air cooling, liquid cooling, as in nitrogen and helium, just to name a few."

"Which one would keep it the longest or be the easiest?"

"My vote would be the nitrogen. It's not the cheapest, but it's very effective. As long as the solid/liquid/gas ratio is perfect, it could last many years, maybe decades or even longer."

"Man, I've got to find out what we're dealing with."

"I've checked with Poisondex and the Chemical Abstract Service, but these three phytotoxins are not registered with them. I've sent out samples to ICCA, the International Chemical Classification Agency in Sorbonne, France. They just might have these phytotoxins in their advanced You see, for three to four months every year, ICCA sends scientists down to the Amazon rainforest in South America and the Congo Basin in Africa to document the various phytotoxins and other derivatives for their medicinal purposes. They're logged, documented, identified, named and studied for their individual properties. ICCA is our only hope."

"Are you telling me that these phytotoxins that are in this formula weren't yet discovered by modern science?

Edgar shrugged. "I don't know. They may have, but it's a long shot."

"Then how do you know there are three of them?"

"It's all in the DNA, my boy. Every living thing on this planet is considered a eukaryote. All of these habiliments have deoxyribonucleic acid in them except for a minute few that only have ribonucleic acid or RNA in them. DNA is found by excoriating the chromosome, thus showing the hereditary material of each original being."

"A basic explanation would've done me just fine."

"I know, but I've always wanted to teach, and since you're my only pupil, you get the brunt of all my knowledge."

Jack cracked a half smile. "I'm all ears."

"To answer your question, the reason I know it's a phytotoxin is the way the body breaks it down. Phytotoxins are broken down along specific DNA channels. Even synthetic chemical compounds have to possess key molecular configurations of an original composition in order for them to work. It's all in how the body metabolizes the elements."

"Wow, you can get all that information from an autopsy?"

"The body is a remarkable machine. It can tell you a lot once you get inside it. Not to mention all the results from the various tests that we perform. With new ones coming out every day, we're more thorough in our examinations."

Jack felt cryptic. *Being inside a dead body, yuck! I'll stay an agent.* "Well, my body's telling me it has to do something it doesn't want to do."

"What's that?"

"I've got to inform Governor Jonathan Woodbine and his wife that their only child is dead, most likely murdered, and that's not even the worst part of it," Jack retorted. "I have to divulge to them the condition Carlton was discovered in. That he was half male and half female."

"I don't envy you."

"Right! I mean, how do you prepare yourself for that? I've got to tell a family that their only offspring will need to be in a closed casket so his relatives won't see him, let alone the press who'll be crawling around trying to snap a convenient photo. It's not beneath them to sneak in and open the casket. Not to mention the scrutiny this case will be under, especially during a reelection year. Everyone will be watching how this will unfold. I'll be getting it from all sides. I'm not good with bad news."

"That's going to hurt them."

"Ouch!" Jack twitched. "It'll hurt me."

"Now you know why I became a Coroner. No fuss—no muss."

"Speaking of a fuss, thanks for all your help. I couldn't have navigated my way around this information without you." He stood up and patted Edgar on the back. "Don't forget to call me when you get the results on those phytotoxins."

"That's if I get the results back."

"Please, think positively."

"I'll positively call if I get the results back. Better?"

"Much better!" Jack sported a hearty grin. "Let me get a copy of the reports so I'll have the correct spelling of those easily-spoken words just in case I've got to look them up or give them to somebody else. I might have to put them in my report. Director Weaver likes everything by the book."

"I know your Director," Edgar said. "I've worked with him a few times."

"So you know what I mean."

"I do."

Once Jack received the needed documents, he shook Edgar's hand and left his office. As he walked down the stairs, Jack came to the realization that extra help was needed on this case. He'd have to go outside the Brotherhood for this added assistance. He opened a hallway door and strolled into the men's room to wash his hands. Touching things in Edgar's office always grossed him out.

He turned the faucet to scalding hot, emptied several squirts of soap into his hands and vigorously rubbed them together. He rinsed them, tossed some water on his face and grabbed a sanitary towel out of the dispenser to thoroughly dry everything.

Jack gazed at his reflection in the mirror. He leaned in and peered at the gray hair that invaded his sides. It had now reached his temples. *This case will probably add more.* Being a year older, he wasn't a spring chicken, but a fallen rooster? No way. That notion was swiftly shaken off. *I need to get over it, just not today.* After stepping back for an overall view, he turned, opened the door and left.

He arrived at his desk and looked for Blaine. Agent Michaels wasn't around. He walked about further. *Why is it so quiet?* He stopped. *Now I remember. Most of the guys are on that case in New York City or keeping an eye on those two malls. I will definitely need to get some help now.* He entered the lunchroom, went over to the far corner where the vending machine stood and leaned his forehead against the glass. *I should call Raymond Davenport and bring his team in on this case. They helped before and they can do it again. I just don't want any bureaucratic flack this time. Just the same, I need the reinforcement. They can do things within the yellow tape that doesn't require all the red tape.*

Jack stared with wetted lips at the candy bars, potato chips and other snack items that were all horizontally held by a metal bar. He was hungry, even ravenous to the point of eating everything inside. He knew that wouldn't be a good move, but reached into his pockets and pulled out some loose change. Several coins dropped and rolled under the snack machine. *Well, those are wasted, and so were three lives. I mean four. All for some bizarre science project. Carlton Woodbine is dead. That I sure didn't need. Then again, neither did his parents.*

He raised his head and snapped his fingers. *That's it. I'll get Governor Woodbine to hire them. Why didn't I think of that before? The governor and his wife would definitely want to know all the details surrounding their son's disappearance and subsequent death. They'd demand it. That's what I'm going to do before his case runs on empty.*

Jack peered back through the glass and eyed more snacks as his stomach rumbled. *I need something to eat before I run on empty.* He looked again. *I know what I'll get.* He put money into the machine, pushed two buttons and watched the freeing of his favored snack. Down slid a granola bar.

Chapter 6

‘ Paranoia can be a man's best friend or his worst enemy!’ At least that's what his old man used to say. Henry knew this well. He lived with it at home and worked with it during the day. That was, until his eighteenth birthday when his dad threw him out of the house. "It's time to leave the nest and learn to live on your own. My pops did it to me, and look at the success I've become," was all the fatherly advice he was given when the door slammed shut.

It was a learning curve indeed. He was the sole heir to Prescott Chemicals a few months later. Working for his father since the age of thirteen, he acquired all the business acumen that was needed, especially what was used to exterminate a rat.

Buford had gotten him out of a several complicated situations, and knew he would again. *I need to move this formula out of here.*

With a fixed grip, the top was unscrewed from a bottle of JD then poured to the rim of his tumbler. *Logan knows more than he's letting on.* Henry gulped down half his drink, clutched the receiver and punched a couple of buttons. It rang.

"Hello."

"Buford, come to my office and don't drag yourself along. Just drop what you're doing and move it!"

"I'll be right there."

Henry hung it back up. *I need to calm down.* He sat back, took a deep breath and thought about what had taken place. Things were a mess, and most likely they'd get messier.

A soft tap came upon the door.

"Get in here, Buford," Henry grunted.

"You wanted me."

"Yeah, take a load off."

Buford sat down. "Is everything all right?

"Does it look all right to you?" Henry barked.

Buford sunk down in the chair. "No, I guess not."

"I agree. So after talking with Logan Price, I've come to a major decision," Henry tossed back the rest of his drink. "He's got a lady friend that needs a job, so I'm going to offer her a consulting position. She'll be helping you on TB4711."

"What?" Buford groused. "Does she know what we're up to?"

"No, this woman doesn't know anything about the plan, and I want it to stay that way," Henry demanded. "All she needs to know is that you need help perfecting a formula. Do you understand?"

"Yeah, but how is she going to work on something without knowing the end results?"

"You both are chemists so I'm sure you'll be able to guide her through the most crucial part of the formula. The one that you're having all of the difficulty with."

"She at least needs to know about the synthetic chemicals I've been using. The FDA took one of them off the market for its negative side effects. She has to know that I have the formula to make it. What do I tell her then?"

"That's your expertise, not mine," Henry specified. "With all the bold-faced lies I've told over the years, you'd think there would be a lot of them stored up in that balding noggin of yours."

"I know what to do. I'll give the drug a fictitious name so she won't know what it is. It's not likely that this chemist is going to

83

waste time isolating its compounds. I'll just keep her busy with the natural end of things."

Henry snickered. "See what an evil mind can achieve once there's a plan of action involved?"

"I just wish you would've gotten a male chemist," Buford reacted. "I can't handle working with a woman. They get emotional easily, and go haywire once a month. I'd rather do this on my own. I'll achieve the final result, you'll see."

"No, you see!" Henry pointed his finger. "I've already made my decision. Besides, there are four dead bodies out there, three with our chemicals in them. I wanted the formula perfected today. Logan needed it done yesterday. It won't be handed to him tomorrow either, will it?"

Buford lowered his head.

"I thought not...so I've decided that no traces of this solution can be found at Prescott Chemicals. Something just doesn't feel right."

"You're not thinking about ditching it, are you?"

"No, I was thinking about selling it as homemade lemonade to all the kiddies at the church bizarre this upcoming Sunday."

"What?"

Henry huffed. "I need you and Arvin to take the small tanker truck, hook up the red hose good and tight to the spigot and backflow the formula into it. Then you two can haul it over to Harold Downing's farmhouse."

"Where?"

"Are you going to ask when, why and how?" His voice boomed. "Harold offered the use of his underground bunker to Arvin and the members of his militia group. They've been storing their shotguns, rifles, automatic weapons, ammo and whatever else they can beg, borrow or steal. I talked to Downing and the bomb shelter isn't just for M.A.G.O.C. He'll let me use

84

it too. We also have use of the distillery that his pappy put in for making moonshine and other spirits during Prohibition."

"Why haven't I heard about this place?"

"Because your job is to redo this formula, not to reload a rifle."

"Are we moving the whole outfit there?"

"Downing's distillery already has a spigot, flow valves, heating units and a few other items I've never heard of. Your pickup has a cab that'll camouflage anything. Take the computer and whatever else is not nailed down, slide them onto the bed of your truck then follow Arvin over to Lysander. Since Harold's tin can is much smaller, you can maybe drop in about a third of the formula. Whatever's leftover downstairs will get the button."

Buford stood up. "What're we supposed to do with the tanker truck?"

"As for that, have Arvin follow you to the old campgrounds. Head in about a hundred yards and you'll see an old broken-down shanty on the left. Park behind it and remove the license plates. Get in your pickup, drive through the woods until you come to Dead Creek Road and head back here."

"Well, I better go call and tell him this bit of good news."

Henry knew Buford hated to be ordered around, but this was inevitable. "I don't take delight in sounding like an evil taskmaster. Nobody wants to deal with a tyrant. This just needs to be done."

"I know," Buford muttered. "Are you done?"

"Make sure to get all those other chemicals and whatnots from the laboratory. Bring them with you and Arvin."

"To the farmhouse...right?"

"Evil minds do think alike!"

"So I've heard." Buford's head hung as he shuffled toward the door.

"Wait! Hold a moment."

He stopped. "Is there more?"

"Yes, so get over here and have a seat."

Buford schlepped toward him.

"I didn't mean to be so unreasonable earlier." Henry knew he could get around Buford's contempt for him without actually apologizing. "It's just that Logan's riding me hard over this damn formula and my temper has reached the boiling point."

"As long as I'm not badly scalded in the process."

Henry cracked a slight smile. "We've been friends a long time. You're like a brother to me. I've never had one." A drab expression fell over his face. "You know I inherited this company when my father died unexpectedly. I took on the responsibility at a young age, and felt the burden of making it successful. It's been ingrained in me from birth. I am my father's child. Hence my temperamental personality."

"A lot rides on your shoulders, and sometimes you need to unburden them. I get that," Buford uttered. "I do that with Arvin, but I know when I've pushed him far enough."

Henry got up from his chair, walked around the large cherry desk and leaned against it. "Remember when I had the idea about an all-natural insecticide, and how we went down to the Amazon rainforest after our trip to Guyana to check it out? You wanted to go there so bad, so I surprised you with it."

Buford grinned.

"You were so excited. I'd never seen you like that."

"I really got excited when I met that reporter, Simone Wellington. I liked her."

"Yes, you most definitely liked her. You followed the poor girl everywhere."

"I'd have drunk that poison if she asked me," Buford admitted.

"I'm sure she came close."

"All went well in the end."

"When you left, and she was rid of you," Henry jested.

"It's not something to joke about!"

"Fine!" Henry threw up his hands.

Buford stood quiet.

"How about when we arrived in Brazil?"

"I liked it."

Henry chortled. "Liked it? You loved it!"

"I did."

"I couldn't believe how beautiful it was."

"And what about the Amazon rainforest? Wasn't that enormous?"

"I'd hate to get lost in there," Henry reacted. "Although, there was a stillness that surrounded you, as if you're the only person on the planet."

"Except when those screeching birds came along…" Buford flinched. "They gave me the willies."

"Thank the sweet Lord we were on a guided excursion." "Yep, what I remember is the fun we had researching the new plant life to create our own green pesticide so we could save the world."

"You drove that guide crazy with all of your questions." "How else was I going to know what to collect?"

"Then came nightfall and we pitched our tents. I took a heaping breath of air before I went to sleep," Henry revealed. "I knew it would put me right out, and it did."

"Until we heard the beating of those drums. That got us up!"

"Yes, we scurried so fast to our guide's tent, asking him what was going on. We were surprised to find out it was the Mayapo natives that lived deep in the woods."

"Remember, we snuck in through that clearing and hid among the bushes to watch them? Some sort of ritual was happening."

"They had that big cauldron over those huge flames boiling God knows what type of concoction."

"Then they performed that mind-boggling experiment." Buford's eyes widened. "They forced those young boys to drink the potion which caused them to turn into women."

"That's the most astonishing thing I've ever seen." Henry flung out his hands "The way they morphed in front of us, right before our very eyes. That was such an awesome feat. What an incredible experience."

"It was amazing."

"Remember, when we were flying back to the states, I said I'd do some reading on the Mayapo natives and their folklore to understand what went on."

"Yep."

"I called later and told you that I'd read how this tribe was known for praising women as goddesses because of their procreation abilities." Henry prattled on. "I still cannot believe they had created some formula to use on those boys who were reaching puberty to change them into females!"

"Yeah, then we discovered what their real purpose was."
"Hell, with no adult males being let into the tribe, they had to keep their population strong somehow."

"Obviously, sex was out of the question, or maybe they did it with each other."

"Maybe they didn't want to be controlled by men." Henry remarked. "Either way, the book I read stated these natives would grab prepubescent boys from neighboring villages and change their sex."

"Crazy, huh?"

"How crazy was it when I suggested we take some of the formula back to the chemical plant, so it could be analyzed to make our own man-made form of it?"

"Quite, until I did some testing and found out about the formula's unique properties, and how it could not be synthetically reproduced."

"Yes, I remember that dark day. I was nervous that we did all of that dangerous crap only to come home with defective crap."

"I also remember what a nervous wreck we were sneaking into their camp to snatch some of that elixir to put in our industrial-sized thermoses," Buford uttered. "It stank so badly."

"Yes, and we dumped out our coffee. What a mistake! I was a mess coming off of the caffeine that entire time. Talk about the shakes."

"I thought the natives were going to wake up and capture us. They would've made us drink it. Thank God we got our tails out of there alive, and with samples."

Henry paced the floor. "It's been over seventeen years since I've put the formula on liquid nitrogen to keep for future use. Well, it's now the future. It's time to put it to use."

"Yep."

"Speaking of samples, how is our natural insecticide coming along?"

"It's coming along."

"That was the whole idea of going down to the Amazon rainforest in the first place," Henry stated. "I only threw in Guyana at the last moment because that's all you talked about was the twentieth anniversary of the Jonestown Massacre and how it would be great to see what everything looks like now!"

"I know. I appreciated it!"

"I know too. Your saying thank you to me constantly for the next two weeks was driving me nuts."

"Yeah, I went a little overboard with that," Buford quipped.

"A little doesn't even scratch the surface."

"Are you going to keep reminding me about that until I'm on my deathbed, or will it stop when I'm under several feet of dirt?"

Henry exhaled. "When my dad was on his deathbed, he touched my hand and asked me to move in closer. I thought my old man was going to finally say something sappy, like maybe he was sorry for throwing me out of the house or that I made him proud. So I put my ear close to his dry chapped lips and he whispered..." He paused and stared into space.

"Your father finally said that he loved you."

"Loved me..." His mouth foamed. "He had never told me that as a child. What would make you think the cantankerous bastard would say it now? He was a nasty ruthless man with no heart whatsoever."

"Really?"

"Foul-mouthed and bad-tempered ruled his world." He wiped the corner of his lips with a couple of fingers. "When he came home drunk, one could expect a belligerent mood. Most times, he never came home at all. But the nights when he did were pure hell. He'd beat my mom mercilessly if something was out of place or dinner wasn't warmed to the perfect temperature or she bought the wrong beer, which he always drank anyways. When the screaming became so bad at night, I covered my head with three or four pillows so it'd drown out some of it. Even

90

now, when I go to bed the screams are in my head more times than not." Henry turned around and picked up his wife's picture. "The saddest part is I became him."

"What do you mean?"

"Never mind, he's not even worthy of the air I breathe." Henry placed the frame face down on the desk and sat down in his comfortable swivel chair. "He was an evil, vengeful man, but I took care of him."

"How?"

"That codger would bring in the same ragged bag with his lunch in it." A loathsome expression covered his face. "It was always the same thing. A peanut butter and jelly sandwich with some crackers. I decided that the rodenticide we made here at the plant would add a little flavor to an otherwise dull routine. I'd sprinkle just a smidgeon daily over a period of time until he finally was on his deathbed." His teeth gritted.

"Could I ask a question without upsetting you?"

"Probably not, but give it a shot."

He breathed out. "What did your old man whisper?"

A distorted look came over Henry's face as hearty laughter thundered out of his mouth.

Buford began to chuckle along with him.

When the calm finally settled in, Henry wiped away his tears of joy. "I really needed that!" A chortle escaped now and then. "With all the stress lately, that couldn't have come at a better time."

"Would you let me in on the joke?"

"My joke of a father whispered in my ear that he had the recipe for an all-natural insecticide/pesticide hidden here at Prescott Chemicals. He told me where it was and to follow it to the letter." Henry sneered. "As old Dicky Prescott lay on his deathbed, the thought of money still lingered on his mind. I have to give it to him. He did have some gumption."

"We do too!" Buford declared. "We've got two projects going at the same time."

Henry rose again and leaned against the side of his desk. "How is GNX969 doing? Henry asked. "I can't wait until we can call it GENEX."

"It's doing," Buford responded. "I'm waiting on FIFRA, FEPCA, the EPA, the USDA and most likely the DEA. For the most part, the primary agencies have kept me in the loop with positive feedback. It shouldn't take too much longer."

"I've been out of the loop for so long that I forgot what the first two anagrams stand for," Henry confessed.

"That's what I'm here for," Buford remarked. The first one is FIFRA, the Federal Insecticide, Fungicide and Rodenticide Act. The second is FEPCA, the Federal Environmental Pesticide Control Act. Each of them has subdivisions that need to be involved. They've taken hundreds of samples of the cuttings and the formulation to be analyzed for safety, efficacy, stability and other needed elements to make sure the product really does what it's supposed to do."

"That's prudent and cost effective."

"Yeah, since bribery and kickbacks allowed unsafe medications and so forth to clog the courtrooms. The greedy lawyers with their class action lawsuits are the ones who benefited from all of this while the governmental agencies got their token slap on the risk. The actual victims received a pittance for their pain and suffering...and the ones who died didn't even get the funeral covered. Swear on the bible then turn the other check. That's the good old American way!"

"You do whatever they ask. I want everything done by the books."

"I do everything I'm asked and more," Buford added.

"Well, we've still got a lot of work to do. I need you to tell Arvin there's a meeting here tonight at 10:00pm. Logan Price is driving down from Washington, DC. It'll just be the four of us. Go now and remove all remnants of the formula."

"I'll get right on it." Buford hurried out the door.

Henry plopped down, opened his desk drawer and grabbed another bottle of Jack Daniel's. After pouring it, he belted back the swig, wiped off his mouth on a sleeve then let out a loud burp.

Chapter 7

The Davenport Detective Agency, established in early 2014, is nestled between two beautiful brownstones in the posh Hiller Heights neighborhood. Its founder, Raymond Davenport, was a decorated police officer who rose to the rank of Deputy Inspector. His position was short lived when he discovered a handful of dirty cops within his squad and turned them in. After being subjected to continual resentment from fellow officers, he decided to leave the force in the Big Apple and move to Washington, DC to be close to his only child, a daughter named Blanche.

Raymond hired three ex-cops from varying backgrounds. Each had outstanding records of personal achievement. They had cleaned out the continuing corruption that plagued their own precincts and had experienced the same harsh treatment. The guys finally left their city jobs for private employment after enduring many bouts of harassment and physical threats.

The first to be recruited was Bren Williams. He hailed from Cambridge, Massachusetts, and considered himself with pride to be the collegiate type. His kept short brown hair was parted on the side. A tight moustache and brown eyes reinforced the look. He labored at the Boston Police Department for seven years before succumbing to the pressure.

Derek O'Rourke, the second detective to join the agency, came down from Cicero, Illinois. Red wavy hair, green eyes, long sideburns and a goatee gave edge to his angular features. He was employed six years with the Chicago Police Department before signing on.

The youngest of the three, Russ Munroe, had hitchhiked from Los Angeles, California. He had a baby-face with pale blue eyes against shoulder-length blonde curls which like, totally sealed his surfer dude status. He worked for the LAPD for five years before his trek to Washington, DC.

Each brought differing methods, strategies and talents to the table. In other words, they didn't always see eye to eye to eye on everything. However, all were in thorough agreement on one very important issue: having one another's back.

"Good morning, the Davenport Detective Agency."

"Hello, good morning. My name is Jack Stanwick and I'm with the Federal Bureau of Investigation. Is Raymond Davenport available?"

"Is he expecting your call?"

"No, but I've something of extreme importance to discuss with him. Will you see if he'll talk with me?"

"Your name again?"

"Jack Stanwick."

"Yes, with the FBI. One moment, please."

Jack leaned back in the chair and put his feet on the desk. He needed their help. A few seconds later, he heard a familiar voice.

"Good morning, Jack, it's been a long time. How are you?"

"I'm fine, Raymond. Can't complain, and even if I did, who'd listen."

"Boy, isn't that the truth."

Jack heard him laugh.

"So what can I do for you?"

"Are you busy with a case at the moment?"

"We're putting the finishing touches on one," Raymond replied. "As a matter of fact, the boys are at the police station issuing statements."

"Well, I think I might need your help on my current one." Jack dropped his feet and leaned forward. "Let me rephrase that. I know I'll definitely need your help on a case."

"I'm all ears."

"Yeah..." Jack jumped up from the chair. He grabbed the phone, raised it off his desk and paced the floor. "I don't really know how to put this?" He honed his thoughts. "The case is very different, or should I say, it's the victim that is. I mean, victims—"

"What're you trying to tell me?"

"I don't want to discuss it over the phone." His volume dropped. "You know the walls have ears."

"Yes, many do."

"You got any free time today?"

"I'm open for the next couple of hours," Raymond responded.

"Oh, good. I can be there in a jiffy."

"I'll see you then."

Jack gathered up the case file, ran out of the Bureau and hopped in his car. *Darn it!* He dropped the case files on the passenger seat. *I forgot to talk to Blaine. Where the heck is he?* He grabbed the cell phone from his jacket's inner pocket and dialed some digits. It rang several times. *He better answer.*

"Hello, Special..."

"Where are you?"

"I'm down in Records," Blaine replied. "What's with the angry voice?"

Jack huffed. "I was just in the office, but now I'm in my car."

"Again with the angry voice."

"I wanted to talk with you a moment."

"Ok, so talk."

"I'm heading to Raymond Davenport's office."

"Why're you going there?"

"Don't worry about that." Jack dropped the visor and looked at his teeth in the mirror. No health bar would show on his pearly whites. "You've got enough on your plate."

"You're not thinking about working with him, are you?"

"What?"

"Man, don't you remember anything?" Blaine groused. "Brass blew a gasket when they found out about it the last time!"

"I told you not to worry about it."

"So you are."

"I'm just getting his opinion on the case."

"Who're you trying to kid? It's Blaine here. And I know you."

"You can't say a word."

"Whoa, where's that coming from?"

"Ah…"

"I'm your partner. Do you really think I'm going to tell somebody?"

"No, of course not!" Jack shook his head. "I'm just under enormous pressure."

"And I don't know this. You're forgetting it's my case too.

I'm better than just filling and filing reports."

"I know, but you've still got to finish…"

"I'm finishing. Besides, if you weren't always sticking me with them..."

"I hate doing them, they're boring."

"Well, it also bores me, but they've got to be done," Blaine countered. "If you helped me, we'd get them done a lot faster. Then you wouldn't need to hire Raymond Davenport."

"I didn't say anything about hiring him."

"Really?"

"Yeah, really." Jack wanted off the subject. "The fact is you're much more studious than me. I'd just mess things up and you'd have to fix them, which doubles your workload." He strived to sell the situation. "I'm helping you indirectly. By my not touching the reports, you can concentrate on them directly."

"Wow, you can certainly pile it on."

"You didn't go for that?"

"No, but a good try though."

"I must be losing my charm."

"Just with me," Blaine quipped. "I don't fall for it anymore, but others still do."

"Good! I'll need to use some on Raymond Davenport. I want him to look at the case file and give me his expert opinion."

"I knew it. He's as good as hired."

"Look, a lot of agents have gone to New York City. The rest are spread thin between counter-terrorism and the recent threats against the President from militia groups over his new gun bill. And you're still doing your thing. I need some help now."

"Well, if you didn't alienate most of the agents here, you'd get people to help you."

"I hate the Bureau's politics and agendas." Jack clenched his jaw. "Not to mention the newbies who want to look the part. The only case they can close is their expensive briefcase, so I stay clear of those morons."

"Well, don't say I didn't warn you."

"Oh, that's good. Jinx me."

"Somehow, you'll get away with it. You always do. You've got that knack of getting people to do exactly what you want. Just look at Simone Wellington for example. She's eating out of your hand."

"Yeah, I know." Jack would never admit that she was such a formidable foe. He considered himself Blaine's role model and couldn't let him down.

"You still there?"

"Yeah, but I need to get going."

"Then go."

"Oh, and by the way, thanks for doing those reports. I know they're not your favorite either."

"Not a problem," Blaine uttered. "I've sort of gotten used to it. I probably get more done without having to fix all your screw-ups. There were so many on the Nicholson case."

"See, I'm doing you a favor."

"Don't do me any more."

"I won't! But do me one. If Simone Wellington calls…"

"I know, tell her to pound the pavement."

"You're asking for it."

"And what, you're the one who's going to hand it to me?"

"In spades!"

"Deal me in."

"Game's on."

"Hit the road, Jack."

"And don't come back..."

"No more!" Blaine hung up.

Jack tossed his cell phone on the case files and drove to the Davenport Detective Agency. After hurrying up the steps and entering through the glass door, he walked up to the receptionist.

"Hello." It was Raymond's daughter. "Blanche, isn't it?"

"Yes!" She gushed. "I can't believe you remembered."

"I never forget a face." Jack sported a grin. "Is Raymond in?"

"Of course, let me tell him you're here." She pressed a button on the phone. "Mr. Stanwick is here to see you."

"Please, send him in."

"Mr. Stanwick, you may go in."

"Thanks, but call me Jack."

She beamed as a chunk of hair twirled around her finger.

He sauntered around the corner and saw Raymond standing at his office door.

"Come in, Jack." His hand was outstretched. "Have a seat."

"Thanks." He walked up and grasped it, gave a manly shake then settled in a chair. "I was thinking about Wisconsin earlier. I can't believe it's been almost two years since we've closed that case. Time sure flies."

"When you get to my age, it seems to soar." Raymond sat down behind his polished oak desk. Jack could almost make out his reflection in it.

"Well, if it wasn't for you and your team, it would've taken me a lot longer to solve. I surely appreciated the help, even if the Bureau didn't give any of you the deserved recognition."

"Just the same, having a low profile is sometimes a blessing in my form of work," Raymond said. "If the boys stay anonymous, they can perform their jobs more proficiently."

"That's true, but if you get publicity more work comes your way."

"It's a catch-22."

"Yeah."

"Between these four walls, Chief Carter has handed us some cold case files to look through. So far, we've closed most of them, which keeps him in a good mood. In turn, DA Griswold is happy that the old caseloads are dwindling. Mayor Burdock is happy because it makes him look good. Even the reporters are happy because the city is safer. Hell, I'm ecstatic. You know I love to work, and the boys, lets' just say they love the money they're raking in."

Jack grinned. "Who doesn't like their paychecks?"

"Well, it keeps the bills from piling up."

"That it does."

Raymond leaned back in his chair. "So what's going on?

I'm sure you're not here to rehash old cases."

"No, I'm not here for that," Jack reacted. "I need your help on a case that's baffling me."

"It must be serious if you're asking me and the boys for help. I thought you received some heat when we helped on the Horoscope Hitter case."

"You mean, when you solved it." He breathed out. "And yeah, I did. It was so unwarranted. I mean, it wasn't me who hired you."

"No, Derek's aunt brought us in when his poor cousin was beaten to death by that maniac."

"How's he doing?"

"He has never discussed it," Raymond replied. "I told him if he needed to talk about it to come to me, but so far he hasn't. I figured he worked it out on his own. It just feels strange to bring it up if he's not dwelling on it. No sense putting it into his mind."

"This is true."

"Everybody has their own way of dealing with the loss of a loved one. Derek is very close to Russ, so they probably have talked it out."

"Yeah, probably." Jack got up from his chair and tossed a large brown envelope in front of Raymond. "Here's the case file complete with photographs."

He opened it and slid everything out onto his desk.

Be prepared. You probably haven't seen this before. I know I haven't."

Raymond picked up the first photograph and gasped.

His eyes bulged outward. "Whoa, Nellie!"

"I told you."

He scanned the rest then lifted his head. "What happened here?"

Jack shrugged. "Now you know why I need your help?"

"My help?"

"Yeah, you and your guys."

"Are you sure you're not biting off more than you can chew?"

"Probably, but I like to eat."

"Yes, but this is going back for seconds."

Jack walked toward the window and stared outside. "Have you seen the Washington Tribune today?"

"Yes, I read it every morning. You never know when it might become my case."

He turned around to face him. "You most likely read the article about the Governor of Virginia's missing son."

"Yes, I did." Raymond nodded. "As a matter of fact, I met Carlton a couple of weeks back at a fundraiser for his father's reelection. What a great kid. He introduced me to his girlfriend, a nice and mannered young lady. I talked with them for half an hour. I can't believe that he's missing."

"It gets worse."

"How?"

Jack stepped toward the desk and grasped a photo. "Our medical examiner told me this is Carlton Woodbine."

"No!" The word lingered as his eyes enlarged.

"Yeah."

Raymond stared at the photo. "I can't believe this." His hand quivered as he held it. "I'm shocked." The head drooped. "I'm in utter shock."

"Me, too."

"Have you heard from his parents?"

"Not a word." Jack sat on the edge of the desk. "I'm sure he's being prepped for his press conference."

Raymond peered at the photo once again. "With Carlton's appearance so—for the lack of a better word—disheveled, the identification must've been confirmed through his dental records."

"They were a conclusive match."

His head shook as it lifted. "Do you have anything to go on?"

"I spoke with Simone Wellington..."

"From the Washington Tribune," Raymond uttered. "What did she have to say?"

"Simone told me about her source and gave me a couple of clues." He pointed. "They're written down on that legal pad."

"Is this gal helping you further?"

"She's supposed to." Jack stood up. "I'm just afraid that she'll be gathering more information from me than actually giving to me." He paced. It always made him think better.

"It's her journalistic background."

"It's her female persuasion."

"You're a smart man."

"She's a shrewd woman."

"Here's a little advice I gave the boys the first day they started," Raymond decreed. "When working with a woman, keep your head in and your heart out."

"Easier said than done."

"What about your men at the Bureau? Why aren't they assisting you?"

"Most of our available agents are in New York City or helping the Counter-Terrorism Division with a slew of newly-intercepted threats. Not to mention the onslaught of school shootings." Jack continued to pace. "Plus, with suicide bombers detonating over four continents and their saying more is to come, our agents are spread thin. Plus, the President's stance on gun control has also ruffled some NRA feathers and those who want to keep their AK-12 assault rifles for hunting purposes."

"What would a person be hunting with a high-powered rifle?"

"That's exactly my sentiment!

"Not to change the subject, but what's been going down in my old stomping grounds?"

Jack trusted Raymond. It was a bond officers had. "Our agents and your old precinct are involved with undercover surveillance work and now about ready to bust the Carmini crime family. RICO indictments will be handed down. Who knows how long that will take? I can't wait for them to come back. I don't have that kind of time on my side. As you know it's a reelection year. This has to be put to rest and fast."

"Let me just say, it's about time the Carmini family were taken down. They have always been a thorn in my side, especially when I worked the beat."

"Well, they won't be pricking anyone, anymore."

"Good!" Raymond smiled. "Now back to work." He held up some photos. "Besides Carlton, are these other two victims also men?"

"All three started their day off as a man."

"Three—that's the number disasters seem to happen in."

"I hope there's only three." Jack knew there could be more. "There's one item I haven't yet mentioned. A fourth victim was found near Carlton. A man, and he was male everywhere. Nothing female on him."

"Are they related?"

"If I was a betting man, I'd say the odds were in my favor."

"Did you have a profile worked up on this psychopath?"

"I gave Benedetti a copy of the case file. Once I hear back from him, I'll let you know."

"I'm sure you ran the M.O."

"Yeah, I've checked all our nationwide databases for anything, anywhere resembling it and came up with nothing." Jack threw out his hands. "When I got home from the morgue last night, I even called several friends that work for the CIA and Interpol, and got zilch."

"Where's the medical examiner's preliminary report?"

"Edgar Cromwell is waiting for callbacks on a few inquiries. If he gets any information, I'll pass it on to you."

"What has he told you so far?"

"That Carlton and the other two men were kidnapped and subsequently injected with some sort of solution made from synthetic and natural compounds."

"Did he break them down for you?"

"Edgar isolated the four synthetic chemicals. He gave me their names and descriptions. The fifth substance, the natural one, has yet to be identified." Jack searched through the pile. "Don't go by the one I wrote. You'll have quite a time with my chicken-scratch." He yanked out a piece of paper, folded it and shoved the thing into his pocket. "Sometimes it's even difficult for me to read. Here's the legible one. I didn't get a chance to make copies of it."

"I'll take care of that."

"The photos are duplicates, so you can have them if you decide to help with the case."

"I don't see any reason not to consult on your case. We enjoyed working with you on the last one."

Jack exhaled. "Great!" His cell phone rang. "It's probably the office." He grabbed and answered it. "Hello..."

"Hello, Mr. Stanwick?"

"Yes."

"Jack..."

"Is that you, Simone?"

"Yes, I need to speak with you as soon as possible and I don't want anybody to hear what I've got to say to you. The other reporters have been circling me like vultures, dying to get a paltry piece of information about the governor's son. May we meet somewhere?"

"Sure. You have a place in mind?"

"I'll be at Fairchild's Café on the corner of Livingston and Grant. Do you know where it is?"

"Yeah, I can be there in half an hour."

"I'll see you then."

Jack shut off his cell phone. *What could be so urgent?* He slid it into his pocket. *Maybe it's another call from her mystery man.*

"Is everything fine?"

"Yeah…" Jack folded his arms. "I've got to meet somebody."

"I'd venture to say it'd be that gal from the newspaper.

The reporter."

"You caught that?"

"Let's just say, when you get to be my age your perception is greatly enhanced."

"Well, you're right. She's got an urgent matter to discuss with me. I hope it's about this case. I could certainly use a break."

"A big one."

"Yeah, now you're talking." Jack grinned.

"I'll round up the boys and give them a heads up."

"Thanks, I was hoping I'd hear that."

"Let's not get our hopes up just yet. From my angle, this case could be a tough nut to crack."

"Any crack in this case is all I'm asking for."

Raymond got up from his chair and approached Jack. "I've got a little ditty that I say to myself when the going gets tough. It sure has gotten me through some tight spots."

"Good, because it couldn't get any tighter."

"It's on a plaque that's hanging in the back apartment." His head dipped to the side. "It says, 'Get ready for the worst and hope steady for the best.'" He smiled and put his hand on Jack's shoulder. "After pondering them, I act accordingly."

"That's some good advice."

"It works for me."

"Speaking of work. If anybody asks, Governor Woodbine hired you." Jack opened the office door. "If I brought you in on this case, I'd be bushwhacked by the brass and that I don't need. At least this way it'll appear clean and my name won't get dirty."

"So we've got ourselves a job?"

"Consider yourselves gainfully employed. Just don't mention it to anyone. I haven't run this by Governor Woodbine yet. I'll break it to him at the press conference. Even so, I don't forecast a problem."

"Here's to good weather." Raymond reached out his hand.

Jack clasped it. "And thunderous results."

Booming laughter gave way, followed by a hearty handshake.

"You better head out before the lunch-hour rush hits.

Otherwise, the two of you will be eating dinner."

"I'm going. I'll leave the files here for you to copy."

"I'll make Blanche personally responsible for that task." Raymond gave an exaggerated wink. "Enjoy lunch."

"Oh, I plan to!" He winked back. "I'll talk with you in a few."

After leaving the office and hurrying across the lobby, Jack dashed down the steps, leaped into his car and sped to the rendezvous.

Chapter 8

The laboratory was quite aseptic, so much so that it would pass any and all white-glove tests. The counters, cabinets, ceiling and floor were snow white. It even smelled like winter. Buford sterilized the entire room after every use. He knew OSHA could drop by on a dime and he didn't want the company to incur a fine on his watch. Henry would kill him...then take it out of his paycheck.

In the middle of the lab was an intricate network of burners, beakers, flasks, graduated cylinders, burets, funnels, clamps, thermometers, stirring rods, goggles, electronic balance and other assorted implements for his experiments. A computer was at the other end for collecting a variety of data.

Buford entered and dropped down on a stool. After picking up the phone, he dialed a number then leaned his back against the wall.

"Yeah," the voice rumbled.

"Hey, it's me."

"Where are you?"

"I'm in the lab pretending to reformulate the formula."

"Let me take the phone in the basement," Arvin groaned. "Ma's driving me crazy."

"She needs another heart attack."

"Yeah, could you help me out?"

"Sure, it's nothing that a little tinkering to her nitroglycerin pills wouldn't fix." Buford chuckled. "Besides, it's not like I haven't done it before."

"Sounds good to me," Arvin sniggered. "I'll bring them there in ten."

"We'll get to that matter a little later. I need to talk to you first about a couple things."

"Shoot!"

"Henry wants you and me to remove the formula from Prescott Chemicals and redeposit it into the small tanker truck."

"How?"

"He had a customized hose made just in case we needed to move it," Buford responded. "One end hooks to the spigot on the vat and the other is screwed to an opening on the tank. The liquid backflows by extraction."

"Isn't there going to be some left?"

"Being that the spigot is four feet from the ground, Henry had configured a drainage system into the blueprint that would be activated by the push of a hidden button," Buford explained. "The titanium floor of the vat will slide in to a chamber and release the formula through a grated base. A unit ten feet above will drop roughly a hundred gallons of saline-treated solution to wash away any residue. All will drain into a pipe that runs down to the creek on his property."

"So where are we taking it?"

"To Harold Downing's farmhouse. Supposedly, he has a distillery in an underground bunker on his property."

"Yeah, he does," Arvin prattled on. "Downing has this huge bomb shelter that his pops and grandpops built around the beginning of World War I in 1914. When the war ended, they shut it down until Prohibition reared its ugly head. They reopened it and built a distillery. Once it was up and running, the family acquired a Ford Model T called the 'Tin Lizzie' and began selling their white lightening to local bars, better known as speakeasies."

"So he was a bootlegger."

"He called himself a moonshiner, and from what I've heard, the whole family was in on it. Supposedly, the men would layer the trunk with the firewater then Harold's grandma along with his Auntie Peg would cover it over with some blankets. The women also put preserves over it to sell at the local stores. Both would drive a thirty mile stretch delivering their wares while the men stayed home to guard the distillery and get drunk."

"That's what I would be doing!"

Arvin continued. "When it became known that the local heat was out in full force, Grandma Downing would put bags of ripped-up paper covered with a few articles of clothing over the preserves and she'd say to the Prohibition police when asked to open the trunk that it was clothes for the needy. She got away with it each and every time. Nobody was the wiser to their operation, even though Grandma Downing and Auntie Peg had on a new dress each Sunday for church. That stopped in 1933 when they repealed that stupid law."

"So they're still using the bunker."

"Well, it's now an underground shelter against the government," Arvin croaked. "I've been to the farmhouse several times. Mostly to drop off items that the M.A.G.O.C. wives have donated. Blankets, canned goods, jellies, jams and a variety of sauces. They also have an assortment of weapons stored in a new room that was built down there. I hear there's a television, several radios and some cots just in case we've got to stay incognito for a while."

"What does it look like?" Buford asked. "How do you get inside there? Who else knows about the place?"

"One question at a time," Arvin retorted. "We're not on Jeopardy!"

"Sorry, I got a little hyper there."

"A little?"

"Okay, a lot," Buford admitted.

"I've only been inside the bunker once. You have to go down into the cellar and enter through a camouflaged door then walk about thirty feet in the pitch darkness. All the while, I could feel myself descending. At that point, a sensor turns on a series of lights. I think I started to breathe again. You know how much I hate the darkness. I wasn't sure if something was going to crawl down the back of my shirt or scuttle up my pant leg. That would've set me free."

"Yikes!"

"Yeah, double yikes!"

"What else happened?"

"As we headed further in, we came upon what seemed to be a dead end. Old straight-faced Harold said it must've caved in. He shrugged and turned around to leave, so I followed him. I'm thinking, is the rest of this going to cave in before we get back to the cellar? Abruptly, he stopped and stuck his hand in some gopher hole. A grinding sound was heard, so I immediately turned around to watch this thick wall of stone move apart."

"Wow, triple yikes!"

"Here comes the quadruple," Arvin countered. "When we entered the room it was huge. Fifty people could be in there at one time. It even had electricity. Not to mention all the creature comforts to make a guy feel comfortable."

"Now that's what I call a man-cave."

"Yeah!" Arvin agreed. "Alcohol maker and all."

"Just don't invite Henry because he'd never leave."

They broke out in laughter.

When finished, Buford asked, "Did the footpath end there?"

"No, we plodded onward to another dead end. This time there was a hidden lever that had to be pulled down for the next door to open up. After walking about a hundred feet, we came to a flight of stairs. Harold reached for the wall and turned this inconspicuous stone. After a cracking sound was heard, these two metal doors moved outward and flattened against the ground by some type of hydraulic source. We then trudged up several steps and came out in the barn right next to an old car."

"It was the Ford Model T, right?"

"You're right, and what a beauty! I inspected every inch. That car was in mint condition. Then came the shocker. Harold asked if I wanted to go on a jaunt with him. Man, I almost crapped my pants, but nodded instead. He drove me from the barn all the way up Swamp Road and back again. That ride was smooth. It was a great eighteen miles."

"Yeah, I'm sure it was," Buford uttered. "Who else knows of this place?"

"I know a few of our M.A.G.O.C. brothers and some of their wives are aware of the shelter."

"By the way, how large is the distillery?"

"You might get a third of the vat in it, but that would be stretching it."

"What do you mean by—stretching it?"

"The thing is ancient and not the sturdiest contraption I've seen."

"I'm not filling it to the rim if that's what you mean," Buford uttered.

"That's pretty much what I meant."

"Do you know what type of material it's made from?"

"I think Harold said copper, but it's definitely riveted together. I noticed that from the get go."

"The good thing about the still being so old is the copper would've been left untreated, which allows the material to form its own oxide layer against corrosion," Buford expounded. "Plus there'll be no leeching of metal particles into our solution."

"What about the rest of the formula?"

"What about it?"

"If Henry is storing the solution down in Harold's bunker, he must know something. Otherwise, why move it?"

"Yeah, I never thought of that." Buford rubbed the back of his neck. "You know, he talked to Logan right before he told me to do this."

"What do you think's going down?"

"Something's telling me that you and I could be left standing there holding the bag."

"Screw that! The only thing I'll be holding are Henry's and Logan's necks while I'm wringing them."

"You need to calm down," Buford requested. "This could just be a precautionary measure in case the FBI come crawling around again."

"I'm not being measured for no pine box when we're given the electric chair. Virginia has the highest rate of kills from the death penalty, and I have no plans on being fricasseed."

"Listen to me," Buford insisted. "There will be no plans made without me hearing about them."

"You wouldn't go to their side against me, would you?"

"Why are you even asking me that?"

"All this business has made me skittish."

"That's the one thing we cannot do," Buford urged. "You and I cannot turn on each other. If you feel something I'm doing is feeling hooky, then tell me, and I will do the same for you. Got it?"

"United we stand. Divided we fall."

"That's what I'm talking about."

"We've been friends for a long time."

"Do you remember how we met?"

"At school," Arvin responded.

"It was in the seventh grade. We both had sixth period social studies with Ms. Jamieson."

"Oh, yeah. She had a great body!"

"After her class, Tommy Gates started bullying me as usual," Buford continued. "He was hitting me in the head with his science book while calling me a dweeb. The other kids just stood there laughing. The next thing I know, you had broken through the crowd, grabbed Tommy by the shirt and hurled him to the floor. All the kids began laughing at him. You told him that if he ever came near your little buddy again, you'd tear his head off and send it home on his skateboard."

"Yeah, now I remember. He wouldn't even walk down the same hall if we were in it."

Buford twisted the phone cord around his index finger. "I don't even know if I thanked you for doing that. It changed my life."

"Knock it off," Arvin declared. "Just coming over to your house after school was good enough for me. I had two older brothers who made me their personal punching bag. By the time your ma served us dinner and dessert, my brothers were out chasing girls and leaving me alone." He cleared his throat. "With you helping me with my homework, I was able to graduate from school. I hated homework!"

"I know," Buford agreed. "As I remember, it wasn't so much as helping you than it was me doing your homework for you."

"One back scratches the other. I had muscles and you had brains."

116

"We worked well together."

"I thought so."

Both men laughed.

"Could I ask you something?"

"As long as it's not about math," Arvin remarked. "That was my worst subject, especially when it came to that guy's decimal crap."

"It's Dewey, and his is used as a classification system for libraries."

"No, I'm talking about Mr. Dooley, the math teacher. I could never understand where to put the decimal mark. I mean, I knew where I wanted to shove it."

"I'm sure you did."

"Being held back in fourth and sixth grade, I never thought I'd ever get out of that building."

"Well, both of us graduated together, didn't we?"

"Yep."

"How about back to my question?"

"Shoot!"

Buford held tight to the receiver. "How much money is Logan paying you for your help?" His voice nearly a whisper.

"He told me to never discuss it with anyone. Why?"

"Because I'm fairly sure he's paying each of us a different amount according to our skill sets. Logan has probably made other promises or incentives to keep us amongst his plan."

"He can't find out."

"Mums the word."

"I'm getting five hundred thousand dollars," Arvin revealed. "It's in an offshore account. Once we complete our mission, he'll give me the account number to the bank and its location."

"Really?"

"At first it was only two hundred and fifty thousand, but after killing Harvey for him he doubled it."

"As he should!"

"What're you making off this deal?"

"A million."

"What? Holy..."

"Shut your mouth about it," Buford ordered. "We cannot let either of them know we've talked about this."

"Do you know how much Henry's getting?"

"No, but I'm sure he's getting more than you and I are making combined."

"Man, that sucks," Arvin grumbled. "We're doing all the heavy lifting and the dirty deeds while Henry and Logan sit back and reap the rewards."

"I'm going to tell you something, but it can never ever be divulged."

"Wow, it sounds top secret."

"Let's just say that friends and family will be left behind not knowing a thing," Buford declared. "You have to promise me on our friendship."

"Okay! I mean, all the numbskulls who're my friends belong to M.A.G.O.C., which I'm tired of babysitting. All of our meetings are full of complaining and nitpicking."

"They will most likely be discovered and disbanded once the FBI and other governmental agencies find out that they we're part of the plot."

"That's for sure."

"What about your family?"

"I only have Royce left since Cletus was killed in Iraq and he lives in Utah with his Mormon wife and kids. I haven't seen him in five years and really don't care if I ever see him again," Arvin stated. "Then there's Ma who I want away from so bad that I'm willing to let you tamper with her medication to put the old broad six feet under or further. So you know what? Yeah, I promise."

"If my plan goes off without a hitch, I'll soon be on the receiving end of a large sum of money, and it's not from Logan."

"What do you mean by large?"

"Ten million dollars."

"Holy Samson and Delilah!"

"Will you quiet down? I'm sure they heard you all the way in Timbuktu."

"Ten million bucks." Arvin calmed down. "Where's that coming from, and how do I get in on it?"

"From a company called Chinow Industries. They're a competitor from southern California and they've already wired the money to an account just below the equator where it's warm year round."

"They're buying some TB4711?"

"No, I'm selling them another concoction I've been working on."

"What is it, and why haven't you told me about it before?"

Buford looked around. "It's an all-natural formula I created," he whispered. "I brought a variety of plants back from a trip Henry and I took to the Amazon rainforest. He swore me to secrecy. I began working on it when you were touring the states with your boxing competitions. It wasn't until you retired and came back here to live that we reconnected. I had to make sure I could trust you."

"You know I can be trusted."

"I know, that's why I'm telling you."

"So how did this company find out about your discovery?"

"I might have let it slip to my old college roommate that I had a patent on an organic insecticide/pesticide that would replace the harsh poisonous chemicals that are currently used," Buford uttered. "I faxed him all my data to date including the findings of the United States Department of Agriculture; better known as the USDA. They have to make sure the formulation passes both FIFRA and FEPCA regulations..."

"Who?"

"Do you really care?"

"No!"

"Anyhow, the Environmental Protection Agency, or EPA, also looked at the reports. The only ones who've so far kept their noses out of it is the Food & Drug Administration."

"That's shocking," Arvin proclaimed. "Usually the FDA has got their foot on everybody's neck making sure they get their kickbacks."

"What's there not to love about corrupt governmental agencies?"

"I'd love to put my foot right up their greedy..."

"As far as that goes, the future will bring us to some exotic island where none of them can get their grubby hands on our tax-free money. As for the present, it is business as usual until my preparation is approved."

"How're you doing all of this with Henry's eagle eyes roving about?"

"My nephew, the lawyer, set me up with his friend who's a patent attorney," Buford retained. "This guy wrote me up two separate patents. One being the actual paperwork that I filed, and the other was a bogus set that I gave to Henry. He's under the impression that everything is coming along just fine. What he doesn't know is the new product will be publicized globally by another company and he'll be left holding his fake patent with no legal leg to stand on. It's just mine. Prescott Chemicals is not mentioned anywhere on the contract. Chinow Industries will be the company that formulated it. I've been an employee on their roster for several months, and since I haven't signed my new contract with Henry due to his head being shoved up Logan's ass, it'll all look copasetic. The damn man should've looked to make sure I had my John Hancock on his old contract that shows I've never had a raise since day one!"

"You are one smart cookie."

"Who could be beaten into tiny crumbs if Henry finds out what I've been up to?"

"Don't worry about him. He can be roommates with Harvey Welch and his three pretty girlfriends at the FBI morgue."

Both men sniggered.

When finished, Buford again looked around. "There's more..."

"Yeah?"

"Prescott Chemicals bought that old run-down greenhouse over on Hinckley Road and had it refurbished. I've been growing all of the natural plants there. Our climate here is too cold for them to survive. I've become such a green thumb!"

"Do you take the plants to Prescott Chemicals to make your formula?"

"No, I had a room built off the back where I take the cuttings to make my preparation," Buford countered. "The excursion guide showed me a method to trim them so they will keep growing, and also how to harvest the seeds for future plants.

Henry became bored and walked away. That's when the man gave me the recipe. I folded it up and stuck it in my shoe to bring home with me. I now mail the seeds to my old college roommate and he brings them to the rival company to grow."

"Doesn't Henry say anything about it when he goes there?"

"He's got too much on his plate to care about the project. That's why he left me in charge," Buford crowed. "Besides, I had all the locks changed so he couldn't get in if he tried."

"Won't that piss him off?"

"If he says anything to me, I'll tell him my keys were stolen at Prescott Chemicals, so I had new locks installed just in case somebody was on to us."

"Who else knows about this?"

"Just Henry and me, and now you. I've been working simultaneously on both formulas. One for good—the other for evil. I was even allowed to choose the identification code for the organic preparation."

"So what did you pick?"

"Since my parents are dead, I based it on my only sibling's name and birth date. It's Mary Jane Sutton and she was born on March 17, 1962. She'd kill me if I told anyone the year of her birth. Why do women get so snarky over their birth year?"

"Beats me."

"It's only from the ages between forty and seventy that you can't ask them their year of birth." Buford sneered. "After that, they'll tell you without even asking."

"Yeah, Ma tells the postman every year how old she is, followed by, 'Do I look it?' He always says the same response, 'You don't look a year over sixty.' It makes her day."

"Anyhow, back to your question. I dropped the year and came up with MJS317. Now I just have to wait on the USDA's completion of the final stages. Then it will be labeled Organix."

"That's a great title!"

"Yeah, my being able to name it was written into the first part of their contract that I placed my signature on," Buford added. "Once I hand over the approved paperwork on the formulation, I'll sign all rights over to Chinow Industries. At that point, I'll be given the account number to the ten million dollars then it's off to my tropical designation."

"Hey, what about me?"

"You're my partner in crime, my best friend. Of course I'm bringing you with me. That's a given. Starting now, our friendship should look somewhat rocky in front of Logan and Henry."

"Do you want pebbles or boulders?" Arvin quipped.

"Just some stones here and there, but more here than there."

"What if Henry does find out about our plan?"

"That's where you'll come in," Buford noted. "Remember, you're the brawn and I'm the brains."

"He'll need to go by way of Harvey. One punch—lights out. It worked great."

"No, I'll take this one. I want it to look like a heart attack or some other physical ailment."

"Why not inject him with TB4711 and let nature take its course?"

"Better yet, I'll spike his Jack Daniel's with it." Buford snickered. "He has never gone a full day without swilling some of that down. I've seen him guzzle it right from the bottle."

"If Henry does have to be taken down, I'm going to bury him out back in those damn woods. He was always hollering about not putting anybody's body on his property. Now, he'll be the only one there—face down—so he can keep both eyes on his rotten land."

"While they're rotting out!"

Boisterous laughter busted forth.

"What's so funny? Henry barked.

Buford jumped up. "Nothing!"

"Is that Arvin you're talking to?"

"Ah...yeah."

"Tell that damn knucklehead to get over here and get this job done!" Henry swung around and stomped out of the laboratory.

"I'll have no problem taking that one out," Arvin declared.

"I would stand back and smile while that miserable fool is placed into his final resting place to rot," Buford uttered.

"And it won't take long," Arvin stated. "He's already rotten to the core."

Buford smirked. "He'll soon be a rotted corpse."

Both chuckled as they hung up the phone.

Chapter 9

Jack pulled up to Fairchild's Café, a quaint eatery on the edge of Dominion Park and parked curbside. All six feet of handsome opened the front door and strode in. From hair to Hush Puppies, he exuded masculinity. He stood and soaked in every saturated smell and sweet scent that surrounded him while gals galore gawked his way with wayward eyes and willful lips. Swooning became the order of the day as lurid looks licentiously lusted.

He was slightly embarrassed and hung his head as the blasts of boisterous babble blathered and bantering barks billowed. Constant clashes of caterwauling and clattering chatter cursedly continued while distressed damsels demanded their designated dining destination. Extra effort was essential on his part not to exit the effervescent excitement engulfing the environment.

As frolicking female follies of fancied fuss and fierce fracas fomented the four walls, the feminine figures were forced into a fragmented file. His heartbeat hastened as he headed toward the horde of humans heralding heady howls. Last in the long line, he listened to the lavish ladies of leisure linger in laughter and lively lingo. Pitches of pandemonium and prattle permeated the place. Rambling ruckus ruled the roost. Yakking yarns yammered yawningly.

Jack was never comfortable around women, and a group of them made him extremely anxious. Feeling out of his element, he looked for a lifeline. Finally, a fairly attractive and youthful woman came up to him.

"May I seat you?"

"I'm, well..." He cleared his throat. "I'm meeting somebody. I mean, a friend is having lunch with me." He anxiously ran his fingers through his thick, slightly salted dark hair. "I'm not sure if she's already been seated. Can I take a look?"

"Certainly," she replied. "Have you been here before?"

"No, never have." He quickly scrutinized the room. "I don't see my friend." Jack peered throughout the area and finally found his tempting target. "Oh, wait...there she is." His finger pointed in her direction.

"Please, be seated and I'll have the waiter bring over a couple of menus."

Jack nodded then worked his way through the crowded establishment and arrived at the table.

"Hi, are you Simone Wellington?"

"Yes, I am." She smiled. "You must be Jack Stanwick."

He grinned. "You look just like your picture." His voice splintered.

"I'm sorry." Simone leaned in. "What did you say?"

His mind wrestled. *What did I say?* Rapid heartbeats banged inside his chest. Did he say something offensive?

Jack grabbed the chair and pulled. Nothing happened. *Is it caught?*

Jack tugged again.

It hardly moved. *What's wrong?*

He summoned more strength and yanked. The chair dislodged and slid across the floor with a jarring screech. It sent a shiver up his spine.

The whole room must've heard that. His eyes darted around.

The outcry of hubbub, hoo-ha and hullabaloo hit an all-time high. Nobody noticed.

Jack sat down and dabbed the moisture from his forehead. "I said..." He bent slightly forward. "You look just like your picture."

She seemed pleased. "My hair is much longer now."

"It looks very nice." Jack knew to compliment a woman, especially if she was fishing for one.

"Thank you." A smile brightened her features.

"You're welcome." His grin flashed an immediate attraction. "I should be thanking you for calling."

"Yes, you should."

"Then I should formally say, thank you."

"You're quite welcome."

"Why are there so many women here?" He looked around. "I see about five males and fifty females."

"Yes, the divine dolls, at least that's what I call them," she replied. "They try to outdo each other with their expensive clothes and their even more expensive plastic surgery. They love to come here in packs where each can gossip about another pack. It's their fulltime job."

A smile flared across his relaxed face. Jack gazed into her amber eyes. He knew that color. It was his mother's favored stone and fixed in most of her jewelry.

"So what's this urgent news flash you wanted to discuss with me?"

"I received a phone call." Simone leaned in. "May I ask you something?"

"Sure, go ahead."

"Is the governor's son dead?"

"Dead!" He jerked upright. "Why would you ask that?"

"Well, is he?"

"Ah...no." Jack shifted in the chair. "No, haven't heard anything about the governor's son. I'm sure I would've heard something, being an agent of the FBI."

"Really? That's quite strange, because I've been informed."

"Are you sure your source is right? After all, he could have an ulterior motive, or be setting you up for a fall."

"I didn't say my source told me."

"Oh." His head angled. "I just assumed the call was from him."

"What's the old adage about that word, assume? It makes an..."

"I'm familiar with it."

"Well, I'm familiar with my source, who has so far been correct."

Jack had to squelch the subject. "Let me check it out before you do anything." His tone tempered. "I don't want you to be disappointed by this man."

"I'm used to disappointment. It's part of my job description."

"What? Why's that?"

"Before I became the lead reporter at the newspaper, I had to bide my time." Her face proved rigid. "I was given second, mostly third and even fourth-rate stories to cover. Not to mention my boss and other male coworkers treated me like a secretary. When I wasn't fetching coffee and doing other menial jobs, I'd be the brunt of sexual innuendos or slapping hands away from my derriere. Married men made passes at me while the single guys thought lurid proposals would interest me. My self-confidence became scarce and I began to loathe being a journalist. I felt always on edge until a depressive attitude settled within me, causing my work to suffer. It made me a mess—a real mess."

"What happened?" Repulsion reared in Jack's tone.

"One day there was a shake-up at the newspaper." Her eyes resumed their luster. "My boss was fired because of a scandalous affair with an editor. The person who replaced him was media mogul, Marjorie Maynard, from the New York News. She gave me some great starter stories. When I proved myself, the bar was raised. She honed my abilities and whipped me into shape. After much sweat and tears, I'm finally where I want to be: at the top of my game."

Jack grinned. "Your hard work paid off."

Simone looked down at her lap. "I've never told anybody that—not even my best girlfriend." She lifted her head and gazed at Jack. "You're very comfortable to talk with."

"Yeah?" He inched forward.

Simone leaned in. "To tell you the truth, I haven't dined with a man in such a long time. I forgot how much fun it could be."

"Yeah, I'm having fun too."

The waiter approached "Good afternoon, here are your menus." He handed them out.

They immediately sat back and took them.

"My name is Eric. Can I offer you something to drink?"

"Water with lemon for me, please," Simone replied.

"I'll have the same, please."

"I'll be right back to tell you about our lunch specials." The waiter turned and walked away.

Jack took his eyes off the menu and feasted them on Simone. "Continue?"

"Oh, goodness! I forgot what we we're talking about."

Displaying a devilish grin, he stated, "Your source called."

"Right!" She slid a slender hand under her softly- sculpted chin. "Well, as I more or less stated before, I received another call from the same man who informed me that the governor's son was missing."

"Yeah?"

"This time, he told me the governor's son was actually dead and also about the other two bodies that were discovered in Maryland and then abruptly hung up."

Jack was silent.

"What's going on?" Her tone rang journalistic. "Are there more bodies?"

"You get no information; at least, not yet. That's our deal."

Her expression altered. "Well, Mr. Stanwick, with no further information, I guess this conversation is over." She got up from the table.

Jack grabbed her by the wrist. "Simone, wait!" His eyes begged. "Please, sit back down. I need to say something to you."

She tried pulling away.

He held his ground. "Please."

Simone eased after another tug. She arched her back and sat down. "You better tell me something I want to hear."

Jack felt annoyed. "Per our conversation this morning, we agreed that I'd give you the exclusive story, which you would then print, when this case was wrapped up. What part of our deal didn't you understand?"

Simone picked up the menu. "I understood most of it."

Jack looked at her sideways.

"Okay, I understood all of it."

"Good."

"I'm just impatient. I hate being idle when I've got this killer story." She stopped. "Ooh, wrong choice of words."

"I know, but you've got to relax and cooperate with me. I'll definitely keep my word. Our verbal contract gives you the right to ask me anything, and in turn I'll answer it. This means you can trust me to tell you everything. Nothing will be off limits, and that I promise. But right now, the less you know about this case, the better. You're a journalist at heart, and as such, too much information is like a time-bomb waiting to blow. You want to get the story first; I get that, but you have to do this my way. I know this agreement doesn't agree with you, but that's how it has to be."

"It's just so hard keeping it under wraps."

"Listen, I didn't mean to sound so harsh a moment ago.

I just want you to realize the importance of my case."

"How about calling it 'our case'?"

"As long as you can keep things in perspective."

"I promise!" She placed a hand over her heart. "Boy, you're really keeping me in check."

"If you're going to help me, yeah, I'll definitely be checking. We need to work together, but on my terms!" He emphasized every word. "No matter how tempting, and under no circumstances, are you to print anything pertinent to this case until the proper time."

"That's definitely checking." She smirked. "I'll wait for the proper time, but just so you know, I'll also be checking."

"I've got a feeling there's going to be a checkmate."

Simone smiled. "Yes, and I'm really good at chess."

"Oh, is that what we're talking about?" Jack flashed a spirited grin.

"You tell me."

The waiter placed their drinks on the table. "Do you want to hear the lunch specials?"

Jack peeked over his menu at Simone. "I'm ready to order if you are?"

She nodded. "I'll have the Cobb salad with the low-fat honey mustard dressing, please."

The waiter glanced at Jack.

"I'll take the grilled chicken sandwich."

"Would you like the red potato salad or French fries?"

Jack bit at the top of his lip. "Ah, I'll take the red potato salad, please."

"Good choice, sir." The waiter collected the menus. "I'll put your orders right in." He turned and headed toward the kitchen.

Jack moved in, gung-ho to get going. "Do you have any idea who your source is?"

"I might."

"Really?" Jack grinned. "Tell me."

"Well, back in November of 1998, my editor—the major louse—sent me on an assignment down to Guyana to cover the twenty-year anniversary of the Jonestown Massacre of the People's Temple. As I was gathering information and interviewing individuals, I met a man who was visiting the site. Not only did I discover he wasn't with a news agency, but he had no family member or even a friend among the dead."

"That's strange."

"That's exactly what I thought." Her eyebrows arched. "Supposedly, he was intrigued by cults and their activities and wanted to know exactly what happened. I just figured some people have a morbid curiosity and after that didn't give it much thought. I had a job to do and I was going to do it, and well at that. So, as I went about my business, our paths kept crossing. For a while there, I thought he was actually following me, but then came to the realization that I was just being paranoid and shrugged off the situation."

Jack went into preaching mode. "Yeah, but you should always trust your instincts." He wanted to instill the idea of protecting oneself. "One can never be too careful, especially a woman."

"You're right!" Simone hoisted up her purse and put it on her lap. She plunged her hand in and rummaged about. A few seconds later, she pulled out an item and aimed it in his direction. "That's why I always carry this."

"Mace!" Jack leapt back and almost stood with his hands up. "Be careful with it." His voice rang urgent. "That stuff can easily go off, and quick at that."

She shoved it closer. "I know. Isn't that wonderful?"

"Simone, for God's sake, put it away before you blast me in the eyes!" His back pinned against the chair. "I don't need them dropping to the floor and rolling under the table."

"Fine!" She slipped the canister back into its pouch. "Besides, they wouldn't have fallen out. It's more likely they'd become inflamed, burn mercilessly and hang from their sockets."

He put his hands down. "I don't want that either."

"Okay, I get it." Simone zipped her purse and tossed it to the floor. "Disaster averted."

Jack's heartbeat returned to its normal rhythm. "Since I've dodged that bullet..." He huffed. "Could you quickly give me the gist of what was said over the phone?"

"Yes, that evening in Guyana as I gathered my workload to take back to the hotel room, this same man asked if I'd join him for dinner. I thought to myself, he's definitely following me, so I graciously declined, stating that I was extremely tired from the lengthy day and wanted to go back to my room and take a long, hot bath; plus I had a deadline to meet."

Jack's anticipation increased. "What happened?"

"As I turned to walk away, he asked my name and which paper I was writing for. I tried to look disinterested, but at the same time remaining polite, so I gave him the information. Then he started telling me about himself, which took forever, so I interrupted him with the 'I have to use the restroom' excuse. With that comment, he stopped. I finally turned around, got into my car and drove away.

"Simone, that's very interesting and all, but what does this have to do with my case?" His fingers steadily drummed on the table to the beat of a favored jazz song.

"Let me finish!" Her eyes glared.

Jack raised both his hands. "Alright!" An apologetic expression filled his face.

"Well, during our conversation, I remembered his distinct voice. It was southern, real southern; almost hillbilly-like. He also had one of those country-bumpkin names." She closed her eyes. "It was Bub, ah...Bubba, um..." The head shook. "No, Bu, ah...Bu...Buford. Yes, that's it! His name is Buford."

"Wow, that's great!"

"Wait, I know his last name." She reclosed her eyes. "Let me think. It was..." Her face scrunched. "Hig, ah...Hig...Higgins. That's his name, Buford Higgins. He's from, ah...hold a second, ah...it was, Virginia, or maybe, West Virginia, no...it was Virginia." Her eyes opened. "Yes, I'd swear on it. It's most definitely, Virginia. So this Buford Higgins and his friend were"

The waiter approached with a large tray. "Your meals smell delicious." He arranged them on the table. "May I get you anything else? Perhaps freshen up your drinks?"

Simone placed her napkin onto her lap. "No, thank you. I'm fine."

The waiter looked at Jack.

"No thanks, I'm good." He grasped his napkin and followed suit.

"Enjoy your meals." The waiter strode away.

Jack watched as Simone took a bite of her Cobb salad. *She even chews delicately.*

Simone laid her fork down, took a sip of her beverage and set it back down. Her eyes eventually landed on Jack.

"This salad is to die for." She leaned forward. "Your red potato salad looks mighty scrumptious."

Jack dug his fork in, placed some in his mouth and chewed with vigor. It's definitely delicious. He swallowed. "It's really good. Would you like a taste?"

"Oh, thank you, but I can't. As it is, I'll be taking this salad with me."

He grinned.

"Do you want to taste mine?"

Jack's eyes broadened. "I might be taking mine home too."

She giggled.

"So tell me the rest."

Simone picked up the napkin and wiped the corners of her mouth. "Well, this Buford Higgins and his friend were headed to the Amazon rainforest once they left Guyana. He said something about going on a guided excursion into the dense jungle to engage in some research on the indigenous plant life. From what I gathered, they were on the verge of discovering an organic insecticide. Supposedly, it was going to revolutionize whatever industry both were involved in and they'd be the first in history to accomplish this feat on such a large scale. He went on about the affect it would have on world hunger and how it would make a difference in the life of millions. After a while, it sounded like a speech the President of the United States would give on Inauguration Day."

"He was a real blowhard, huh?"

"You could say that." She picked at her salad. "I tried to ignore him, but he kept pestering me, so I pretended to listen. Basically, I really only heard bits and pieces of his royal rant. I just figured he was some sort of geeky scientist who didn't get out much and wanted some attention from a female. I really felt sorry for him and thought he was harmless."

"In my line of work, it's usually the quiet types who've got the pent-up aggression inside."

"I like my men hostility-free, thank you."

"You'd be surprised what emotional or mental disturbances can produce when violence is added to the mix. I've sat in on the profiling of three serial killers: David Beldoff, Frank Kilpatrick and Tom Wortham. All told how they were cast aside growing up and had been physically and/or sexually abused as children. Their depositions reported on being bullied, beat up in school and even at home. So many pleas for help were ignored by teachers and other authority figures. Not to mention the spurning from the opposite sex...or in Beldoff's case, the same sex. Basically, they've been shut down and out to societal normalcy."

"I read an article about this. Tell me more."

"Well, these men, in their minds, weren't able to have the two-parent home with the white picket fence and a family dog; what's supposedly idealized as the perfect childhood. Even though Kilpatrick and Wortham had two parents, they'd removed that perceived connection from their mind because of the abuse. Instead they recounted a life of mental, emotional and physical abuse, along with deep-seeded pain and suffering."

"That is so sad."

"It is." Jack concurred. "I took a course on criminal psychology and boy, I learned a lot. I was shown how these men, who didn't receive the necessary love and nurturing, developed a void, a hole of sorts that needed to be filled. Instead of getting intense psychotherapy to understand their feelings to these complex issues, each took matters into their own hands and created what we refer to as a psychopath."

"You mean a monster."

"Yeah." Jack agreed. "When I had a meeting with each of them, all three stated—in different terms, of course—that from a young age, something inside them died and something devious was born. I was told that they remembered anger from when they were small children, and the hatred was so bad that just to relieve it, a family member or even a neighbor's pet was killed. It's a resounding theme."

Simone kept her head askew and did not say a word.

"You'll have to forgive me. I sometimes forget I'm with a civilian. I usually eat with workmates."

"That's fine." She sighed. "Sometimes my curiosity gets the better of me."

"Why don't you continue telling me about your source?" He hoisted a forkful of food to his lips.

"Let me think back. I've got to figure out where I left off."

"You were saying this Buford Higgins character was following you around and telling you about some research in the Amazon."

"Oh, yes, the Amazon rainforest." She breathed out. "Buford went on and on about working for this established chemical company in Virginia and that he and his associate—that's how he put it, like I was somehow going to get lathered over his use of verbiage. If he thought it was going to impress me, it didn't work. Anyways, he and his associate were going there to obtain some type of plants, herbs, shrubs or something to that effect and develop it into this world-renowned, environmentally-safe pesticide for protecting crops. He went on to say that his associate owned the chemical plant and he was the lead chemist on the project. It was supposed to be the wave of the future, but I don't even know if it got off the ground—or for that fact—on the ground. We could certainly use it now with the way our ozone layer is being depleted. Global warming is ruining our planet. A year or two back, I researched it for an article that got a lot of fanfare, I might add."

Jack needed to reign her in. "This is very informative and all, but where is it going?"

"You've got to hear me out..." A curt tone echoed forth. "I'm trying to give you some back story."

"Oh, okay!" He threw his hands up. "Geez, I didn't mean to interrupt your back story."

"I'm just saying, it could reveal a clue, that's all. You do need those, right?"

"I do." Jack sat back. "So what happened next?"

"At that point, I wondered when his friend was going to pop up in the picture. I mean, after meeting Buford, I figured there had to be some brains behind this adventure. A short time later, he brings this man over to meet me. His name was Henry Prescott. The reason I know this so well is because my grandfather's name is Henry and my brother's middle name is Prescott. I thought to myself, how uncanny is this? I mean, what are the odds. It's madness, how you can remember things when you go back in your mind. It must be the journalist in me."

"It must be." Jack stroked her effervescent ego. He knew she was giving him a taste of her journalistic prowess. "So you were saying..."

"Well, a few months later, I get a telephone call at the Washington Tribune. Guess who?"

"Buford Higgins."

"Yes." She nodded. "Supposedly, he was coming to Washington, DC in a couple of weeks to acquire a patent on a chemical formula that he and his company were developing. Of course, he asked me if I would escort him around, basically show him the sites and take him out to eat at some of the local restaurants. Naturally, I declined. However, he was persistent. This guy called my office every other day it seemed. I finally had to tell the receptionist not to put him through anymore, and to inform him that I left town on an assignment and I'd be gone an undetermined length of time. The calls finally came to a halt, until now. Buford Higgins is the one calling, supplying me with this information. I'll swear my life on it!"

"I wonder what his motives are."

"Maybe he thinks that by telling me this information, before anybody else, I might want to meet with him or something to that effect. Fat chance! I'll never be that grateful."

Jack lost his appetite. He'd dealt with informers before and knew that they all had more than one reason to speak up. "Listen, Simone…" He didn't enjoy what was about to come out of his mouth. "Next time he calls you, be nice to him. Make him feel that you are interested in what he has to say. Most importantly, thank him for any information he gives you."

"What?" Her eyes shot wide open.

"Create a discussion and garner a rapport with him." He implored her. "Let him feel secure in speaking with you. He has to gain your trust."

"Jack, you're kidding, right?" Simone dropped the fork into her salad. He saw a look of disgust flash on her face.

"I wish I was."

"Thanks a lot, Jack."

He felt her uneasiness.

"If this Buford Higgins is feeling smug, he could slip up and we'll nail him."

"What if he starts to harass me again? I mean, this man could become psycho if he finds out that I'm playing him. If that happens, I might be his next victim."

"No." Jack edged in. "He's only killing men." *That didn't just come out of my mouth!*

"Oh, in that case..." came the obvious sarcasm as she threw her arms out dramatically. "I'm all for it."

"Simone, that came out all wrong."

"You think!"

"I'm just trying to be realistic."

She sat back. "Really, I haven't noticed."

Air flew from Jack's nostrils. "Look, this Buford Higgins character is laying all this information in your lap for whatever ulterior motive. Accept his calls. Whatever's going on, he might be experiencing remorse. Possibly, his guilt is eating at him. I've learned over the years that the conscience is a very powerful tool. It has softened many a hardened criminal. The thing is, he's breaking his silence and you're the professional he's choosing to unload on. Use it to your advantage. This story will be huge when it comes out. Not to mention a break as such could help me immensely. Hey, look at it this way. It'll be in your newspaper first. You'll come off as the media hero."

"More likely I'll be on the front page with the caption: **Simone Wellington Found Bludgeoned to Death in City Gutter**—with a putrid photo of me next to it."

"Either way, you'll still be a media hero!" Jack ducked, waiting to hear her response.

"You fool!" Simone's napkin grazed his shoulder.

He inched his head up, making sure the butter knife wasn't next.

"I think you missed you're calling. You should've been a psychiatrist."

"I'm a much better agent." He bared a slight grin.

"Is that so?" Her tone tempered.

"Yeah." Jack stared into her eyes. "So will you help me?"

Simone's expression surrendered. "I'll help you."

"Thanks!" The weight melted off his shoulders. "I really appreciate it."

"Don't mention it."

"And don't worry, there's no way this character will get anywhere near you. The FBI will guarantee your safety. I'll see to that. Just stay relaxed."

She nodded. "What will I do? I mean, when he calls?"

"A trace will be installed and a small black box will be attached to your work phone. If Buford calls from a landline, a green light will come on. Keep him talking. It'll take sixty seconds to run his locality. If he uses a cell, an orange light will pop up, but that's even better because the spoor will establish what tower the ping originated from in seconds. It'll also initiate a tracking equation from a remote coordinate grid that'll compute his trajectory and we'll be able to hone in on his exact whereabouts. In the meantime, agents will sequence our state of the art Pitch Detection System to compute his voice. It'll then be streamed against previously recorded wiretaps to gather whether he's part of any illegal activities. If so we'll nail him."

"Wow, technology has certainly come around full circle."

"It definitely has for governmental authorities." His confidence on full display. "Look, if for any reason you want to leave the investigation, just say the word. And if things get too dangerous, I'll pull you out and send you on an assignment for an extended period of time until we catch him. Either way, you're my top priority."

She snickered. "The Witness Protection Program—here I come!"

The waiter approached the table. "May I get you anything else?" He focused his attention on Simone.

"No, nothing for me, thank you."

"Not even dessert?" He tried to entice her.

"No." Her head shook. "I'm stuffed."

The waiter turned toward Jack. "What about you, sir?"

"No, thanks. Just the check, please."

"I'll be right back with that, sir."

After the waiter left, Simone picked up her purse. "Well, I need to get back to the office just in case my secret admirer calls." She pulled out her lipstick and applied it as she stared at the back of a spoon. "Anyhow, I've got some notes to dictate for tomorrow's edition."

"I hope not about the case." He attempted to be amusing.

"Not with you and the FBI trampling all over my first amendment rights." Her tone sarcastic. "Now can I?"

"I would hardly call it trampling." His eyes tapered. "I'd say it's more of a traipsing."

"Oh, would you..."

The waiter put the check on the table. "Thank you, and have a great rest of your day."

Jack snatched it up and skimmed it. "Hold on a second..." He reached into his back pocket and retrieved his wallet. He dug around in it. "Here you go." He handed over some money. "Keep the rest."

The waiter gave a gracious grin. "Thank you, sir!" He scooped the slip and money off the table and walked away.

"I think you made his day." She casually glanced at Jack's wallet. "An heirloom?"

"Granted, it's old and beaten up." He slid it swiftly into his back pocket. "I've been meaning to get another one. I just haven't had the time."

She smiled and got up. "Thank you, lunch was delicious."

"Oh, don't mention it." He rose from his chair. "Thanks for the heads up. I really appreciate what you're doing for me."

"Just remember to honor our deal."

He winked. "I'll honor our deal."

"Again, thank you for lunch." She put her hand on his arm. "The next one's on me."

Jack endowed a wide-eyed expression. "Our next meal…"

"Of course!" Simone let him go. "We might as well eat while I get the exclusive interview from you."

"Got it!" He nodded. "Oh, by the way, I'll be sending an agent over this afternoon by the name of Stan McCall. He'll be installing the wiretap. It'll have a linked recording device. Before answering the phone, push the red button and it will tape your conversation, just in case something happens."

"As in my demise."

"That'll never happen. I'm making you a solemn promise."

"I'm going to hold you to it."

"I'm hoping so."

Simone spun around and walked as Jack followed her out of the café and to her car. They bid each other adieu.

Chapter 10

Raymond gathered his men together at the Davenport Detective Agency to discuss the case. As they were all crowded around his desk, he knew their casual banter and pleasant laughter would soon be replaced by emotions from the darker side of detective work.

"Guys, listen up."

A hush came over the room.

"It looks to me that we've got one humdinger of a case here in front of us." Raymond tapped his hand on top of a brown envelope.

"What do you mean?" Derek asked.

Russ edged forward. "Like, totally give us the low-down."

"When you see the photographs, you'll understand." Raymond pulled out the contents. "I'm passing around the preliminary case file that FBI Agent Jack Stanwick had gathered for us. You'll see there are three victims. All have been murdered. The thing is their bodies have been..." He hesitated. "How should I say this? Altered."

"Altered?" Bren's eyebrows scrunched.

"Very altered," Raymond decreed. "Agent Stanwick will be calling shortly to discuss everything."

"Like, we're totally working with Jack Stanwick again?" Russ uttered.

Raymond winked an eye. "We're working for the Governor of Virginia."

"Why the governor?" Derek questioned.

"His son is one of the victims," Raymond answered.

He heard the three men gasp.

"I know..." Raymond handed out the last of the file. "I was shocked myself."

"What's going on here?" Derek held up a photograph.

Russ snatched it. "Like, whoa! What way happened to this dude or babe or whatever it is?"

"This dude or babe..." Bren mimicked him as he grabbed the photo and scanned it. "This person must be a transvestite or maybe a transsexual."

"It's so not a tranny." Russ swiped it back. "Like, I should totally know since I've been with one."

"Wow, utterly shocking." A hint of sarcasm resonated in Bren's voice.

"Guys, they're neither." Raymond gave Russ an odd look. "Jack informed me that all three of them were males with female characteristics."

"For real?" Derek queried.

"Yes," Raymond replied. "The photo that Russ has is Carlton Woodbine, the governor's son."

"Like, no way," Russ uttered in his Valley Girl natter.

"Like, yes way," Bren stated again in a sarcastic tone as his head bopped side to side.

"This dude is totally tore up from the floor up."

Bren took the photograph from Russ' hand.

"Like, so give that back to me, you rank toad." He seized hold of it again.

Bren pulled it away then lifted up his finger. "You've had it long enough."

"Like, whatever!" Russ gave him a snarky grin.

"Can I see the photo?" Derek reached for it. "And don't you two start your shenanigans, do you hear me? I'm not in the mood."

"Dude way started it!" Russ eyed Bren.

"Well, I'm ending it," Derek growled. "I'm not babysitting you two today." He held his hand out. "Can I please have the photo?"

"You're not going to enjoy what you see." Bren gave it to him.

"I'll be the judge of that." Derek peered down at it. "Wow, what could've done this?"

Raymond rested both arms on his desk. "The victims had some manufactured drugs in their systems along with some other rare substances."

"What rare substances were found? Bren uttered.

"We're just waiting for the medical examiner's preliminary report." Raymond glanced at his watch. "Jack should be calling anytime now. He'll give us all the facts."

"I can't believe this is Carlton Woodbine." Derek's head shook. "I just saw his picture in the paper last week. He'd gotten into some trouble again with his drinking and the cops were called. He was disturbing the peace."

Bren snickered. "You know he wasn't arrested for his bad behavior. Carlton is the governor's son, which means he's exempt from trouble."

"Like, if that was so one of us, we would've been way jacked into the clinker," Russ quipped.

"It makes me sick that the law plays favorites," Derek added. "If they have clout, just let them out."

"The criminal justice system needs a healthy makeover, and the only way that's going to happen is to get rid of all the money-grubbing, pork-spending, ancient carcasses that have been in the Senate and Congress forever." Bren sneered. "Or for that matter, in all governmental posts, and put some youthful energy there with our progressive ideals in mind."

"Exactly!" Derek piped up. "The majority of them are close to death anyways."

"Like, remove the old ass and bring in the new brass," Russ blurted out. "That's totally my motto."

"I hope you're not talking about me!" Raymond broadened his shoulders.

"No, we're talking about these useless timeworn men who have been drafting bills and signing legislation, which only adds more profits in their own pockets to the detriment of us," Bren proclaimed. "The mindset on the hill is, let's tax the middle class out of their paychecks while the wealthy fat cats in Washington pay nothing. There will soon be two classes: the rich against the poor. It's crazy!"

"You know what's even crazier? The fact that these idiots keep getting elected," Derek remarked. "If it was anybody else who was running a company into the red, they'd be fired, and fast. Not these fools. They block key legislation for farm aid, unemployment benefits, social security payments, and welfare issues, or push them so far away from the current agenda to go on their many breaks, hoping people will forget about them because they're so wrapped up in their daily lives to care."

"Only when our country is bankrupt will they take notice, but that will be a little too late," Bren added. "The people of our great nation need to wake up and realize that we're heading downhill fast. These women-molesting, prostitute-buying, sexting morons who're in our state's capitals and Washington, DC, have their hands on the steering wheel and they're immorally driving us into the ground. We need fresh blood. The stale status quo has to go."

"It wouldn't matter, anyways," Derek continued. "Even if you put some in office, they would be corrupted by the ones who've been there since the turn of the century. Those old crones think they're owed the right to do what's good for them instead of doing what's right for us. Don't think they haven't gotten around the law with their loopholes that they've installed to use our taxpayer dollars for their own gain. I'm sure we've bought plenty of mansions, yachts, vacations, fancy cars and facelifts for them and their families. Why not? It's just another write-off. The IRS wouldn't dare audit one of their own."

"Like, totally!" Russ agreed.

"Why are you going after your own party?" Derek looked at Bren. "I thought you were a staunch Republican."

"I am," he crowed. "I can however be bipartisan."

"I totally can too," Russ blurted out.

Derek snickered. "I think you mean bisexual."

"Like, whatever!"

Raymond laughed. "You three have missed your calling. With those speeches, you should throw your hats into the ring."

"Not me!" Derek fired back. "I'll wring their necks."

"As would I." Bren concurred. "I'd rather arrest them than work with them any day."

"Like, not for sexting, though," Russ uttered. "That's totally up my alley."

Bren smirked. "I'm sure lots of things went up your alley."

"Are you boys finally down off your political soapboxes?" Raymond asked.

The guys looked at one another and did not say a word.

Russ finally broke the ice. "So, how do we totally proceed from here?"

"Jack will tell us how to proceed with the case," Raymond replied. "In the meantime, we must keep this information under our hats, especially what I told you about Carlton Woodbine."

Bren pointed. "You better stare at Russ when you say those words."

"Like, whatever!"

"You were the one who told that pretty reporter about the Crawford case before you were supposed to." Bren kept his finger aimed. "Do you actually think we didn't know who her anonymous source was? Please, you were slathering all over the poor woman."

"Like, again...whatever!" Russ enunciated every word.

"Guys, knock it off," Derek stressed. "I'm really over all this bickering."

"I think you're fighting a losing battle," Raymond countered. "It's unfortunate because in this line of work, a tight team is a powerful team. You boys should look at the wall behind you and see my new plaque."

They turned around.

"I've put it there so you three could see it every day. It reads, 'What lies behind us and what lies before us are small matters compared to what lies within us.' You guys need to take it to heart."

The intercom crackled and startled them.

"Dad, Agent Stanwick is on line one," Blanche announced.

"Thanks, honey," Raymond said. "Are you boys ready?"

They nodded in agreement.

Raymond lifted the phone to his ear as the rest waited in suspense. He pushed the blinking button. "Hello, Jack. I've been expecting your call. My detectives are here and rearing to go. I'm transferring you to speaker. Go ahead."

"Hey, guys," Jack clamored. "Did you get a chance to look everything over?"

"Just the photos," Raymond responded. "I didn't want to overwhelm them until you called."

"Pretty startling, aren't they?" Jack emphasized.

"They're unbelievable," Bren reacted.

Russ twitched. "Like, the photos are way freaky."

"What happened?" Derek enquired.

"First, you will need the case file," Jack replied.

"I've got it right here." Raymond opened his desk drawer, pulled out the photocopies and handed them to his detectives.

"Second, you guys will need to write down the new information I just received," Jack requested. "You probably won't get heads or tails out of my phrasing."

"Go ahead," Raymond issued. "They already have their notebooks and pens ready."

"Like, I'm also recording it," Russ added.

"That's what I like—preparation." Jack sounded out each syllable.

Raymond laughed. "I do too."

The detectives looked at each other as their eyes rolled back.

"Ok, here I go," Jack stated. "The three bodies that you're looking at have been injected with some synthetic and natural compounds that caused them to partially morph from men into women. Four of these chemicals were isolated by our lab. As you can see, the first is a diet medication by the name of Dycilatium. It was used in the 1950s, but was subsequently taken off the market years ago because of the despicable side effects. Now the second is known as Criamazine. It's an anti-seizure/anticonvulsant medication. Our third chemical compound is Triamerisol, which is a preservative to keep the others from going bad. It only has an effect on the chemicals, not the natural substances. The fourth one is Mandrolifid. Its main purpose is to make sure the formula does not evaporate. Edgar Cromwell, our Medical Examiner, has now told me about the fifth."

"So it was discovered," Raymond spoke up.

"Yeah, and it's a dilly," Jack quipped. "I faxed the results, so they should already be there."

"Like, I'll check the machine." Russ jumped up and rushed out the door.

"Whoa, he moves fast," Derek blurted out.

Bren snickered. "Just ask any woman he encounters."

"Boo-yah!" Derek grinned.

Russ hurried back in and passed them out.

"Jack, we're ready when you are," Raymond noted.

"This part is where you'll need your notebooks and pens. Keep that tape recorder running also," Jack requested. "Edgar was informed by the International Chemical Classification Agency in Paris, France, about the items that make up this fifth compound. The ICCA told him they were discovered in 2002 when a team of scientists went down into the Amazon rainforest to collect samples for possible medicinal purposes. This fifth compound is made up of three natural substances that were found on the expedition." He stopped. "Are we all on the same page?"

Raymond looked at the guys. All were writing in their notebooks. "It seems we are."

"Great!" Jack continued. "The first is a plant known to the scientific world as Crobatternum rotsegallam. The second is a shrub called Ingesturnium teraliaous, and the third is a berry known as Filiosturanias permagallus."

"How do they totally come up with these rad words?" Russ issued.

"They're all scientifically branded," Bren responded.

"They're a mouthful," Derek expressed.

"That they are." Jack agreed.

"Did the ICCA say how each of them specifically worked once inside the body?" Raymond leaned in.

"They did," Jack replied. "Edgar gave me the details. The first one can naturally stimulate the estrogen and progesterone process while drastically reducing testosterone levels. The second one revs up the pineal gland in the brain to increase its size and basically tells the body it's time for puberty. The third one can create an endocrinal imbalance of the thyroid gland, which will throw off the lymphatic system, forcing an increase in hormonal changes. All three in combination create this nightmarish effect. Someone has taken all five counterparts and made a natural/synthetic solution to inject into these people to cause this very strange transformation of gender—a kind of metamorphosis."

All was silent as the detectives finished up.

"Guys, did you get all that down?" Jack questioned.

"Yeah, for the most part," Derek answered.

"This is one majorly crazy dude," Russ blurted out.

Bren looked at him. "In this day and age, he'd be called a serial killer."

"Whoever he is, this is one for the books," Jack noted.

"What's our game plan?" Raymond crossed his arms.

"We need to check out the local chemical companies to find out which plant is pumping out these toxic chemicals," Jack replied. "There shouldn't be many in the area."

"I can take care of that," Derek stated. "I'm awesome with a computer."

"Like, he has mad skills," Russ quipped.

Bren smirked. "We're proud of our little geek."

Derek shot him a foul look.

"Cross-reference the companies that make pesticides and insecticides," Jack suggested.

"Got it." Derek made a note.

"Next, a man by the name of Buford Higgins needs to be located."

"I can totally do him," Russ offered.

Bren Sniggered. "You'd do just about anybody."

"Boys!" Raymond reach his tolerance level. "Listen."

"He could be employed by this same chemical company," Jack cited. "Start with Virginia and fan out from there."

"Does he have a rap sheet?" Bren probed.

"No. I ran him thru NCIC."

"What about CODIS and VICAP?" Derek mentioned. "I can check them out."

"How do you have access to them?" Jack asked.

"Don't ask," Bren retorted.

Raymond shook his head. "You don't want to know."

"Yeah, you're right...I don't," Jack maintained.

"Like, how did you find out about Buford Higgins?" Russ uttered.

"A reporter from the Washington Tribune by the name of Simone Wellington called and informed me of this character," Jack replied. "Buford's been calling and telling her about this case. He told her about the disappearance then the subsequent death of Carlton Woodbine. Not to mention details to which the press was not privy."

Bren smiled. "Is that the same Simone Wellington who wrote the article about Carlton Woodbine?"

"Yeah, one and the same," Jack responded.

"Duh!" Derek glared at Bren.

Bren threw him a nasty glance.

"She is mad gorgeous," Russ blurted out.

"Down boy...now heel!" Bren issued. "Is everything about a woman with you?"

"Like, is there anything else?"

"Russ, keep focused on the case," Derek groused.

"You might as well save your breath," Bren remarked. "It's like beating a dead horse."

Russ snickered. "I'll be majorly beating you."

"Guys, you need to stop," Derek ordered.

"Sorry, Jack." Raymond apologized. "You know how rambunctious the boys can get," he added. "You were discussing Buford Higgins' conversation with Simone Wellington."

"I feel he's a key player in this charade," he said. "Simone thought he hailed from Virginia or somewhere down in that vicinity due to his heavy drawl."

"Russ, you'll help Bren in locating this Buford Higgins," Raymond requested. "And play nice."

"I'll totally help him." He rubbed his hands together while a cat-eat-mouse grin flashed on his face.

"Russ…" Raymond warned.

"Like, I'll be cool." He turned and winked at Bren.

"I'll wrestle up the info on chemical companies in that area." Derek chimed in. "Do you have a motive yet?"

"No, I don't," Jack replied. "I'll need your help with that."

"We'll find it," Bren declared.

Russ nodded. "Like, totally!"

"Well, that's the whole of my case," Jack stated. "You can see why I need you."

"We'll handle it." Derek confirmed.

"We've totally got your back," Russ uttered.

"Yes, we do." Bren agreed. "We'll get this guy. It's practically guaranteed."

"Thanks," Jack expressed. "I really appreciate it."

"Not a problem." Derek got up. "I'm going to get on the computer. Bye."

Russ bounded from the chair. "I'll totally catch you later!"

"We'll talk with you soon," Bren added. "Goodbye."

They left the room.

"They're such great guys," Jack commented.

"They are most of the time," Raymond remarked.

"I wish I knew what Buford was up to. All I feel is that something big is about to happen. I just hope we can stop it before it does." Jack exhaled. "In the meantime, I've got to tell Governor Woodbine and his wife about their son. I can't put it off any longer or the department will have my head."

"Have you decided how you'll broach the subject?"

"I'll just give it to him in a direct manner," Jack replied. "I hate beating around the bush. It causes me to stammer in the worst way.

"I would also hem and haw," Raymond added. "Having to tell someone that their loved one is dead—been murdered nonetheless—is the worst experience in the world."

"Wait! How about dead—murdered by a serial killer— and grossly disfigured," Jack countered. "Not to mention all the questions the governor and his wife will have. Then there's the press, who'll play this story to death, and make the Woodbines relive it over and over again."

"I definitely had to develop a strong stomach for those missions."

"Speaking of which, I better get over to the Woodbines before mine becomes ill thinking about it or before they hear any ill-fated news."

"Keep me posted."

"Right back at you," Jack quipped. "I'll talk with you soon. Bye."

After hanging up, he dialed another number and held the phone to his ear.

"Federal Bureau..."

"Hey, Blaine, it's me."

"Jack, my long lost partner! Are you still collecting a paycheck?"

"Yeah, I hope so."

"Well, Weaver's under the impression that you're on the way down to Governor Woodbine's press conference," Blaine stated. "You've got a couple of hours to drive there and prep him for it."

"Did the captain tell him what has taken place?"

"You should do stand-up at the Comedy Club," Blaine replied. "The captain? Tell anybody bad news? I know you're joking."

"Damn! I better rehearse my routine on the way down."

"I would."

"I hate this!" Jack started his car. "I can't deal with people when it comes to bad news, especially if they're crying."

"Have you yet to go over to Raymond's place?"

"I'll tell you all about that later or most likely tomorrow. I'm getting a hotel room so I can professionalize myself for the three-ring circus. Between consoling the Woodbines, dealing with the pressure-angst press and keeping onlookers at bay...I'll be exhausted. Not to mention the drive down to Richmond. You know how much I love the traffic on I-95!"

"Oh, boy, do I." Blaine was sarcastic.

"Do me a favor..."

"You mean like the favor you've done me on the Yarborough case?"

"Let it go," Jack uttered.

"Someday."

"Well, in the meantime, I need you to tell Simone to call me on my cell phone. I want to tell her about the press conference, but I'm too busy to go through that whole rigmarole of looking her up."

"She's becoming a habit."

"One I don't want to break." Jack snickered. "I'm just joking."

"If you say so," Blaine said. "Oh, by the way, when I'm done with all of this paperwork, I'll join you."

"That won't be today."

"Or tomorrow either."

"How about I trade you?"

"No way," Blaine retorted. "Sayonara."

Jack sighed. "Shalom."

Chapter 11

J ack scoped the Governor's Mansion from a distance through a row of Southern red oak trees. Barely a leaf clung to the twisted branches as squirrels played happily on them. As he drove closer, the four white pillars that kept the massive brick structure upright came into view. Its majestic splendor was untouchable. The once manicured lawn was now invaded by an oddity of people who came to gawk and gape at the stricken family. How the mighty have fallen. Nobody would fall as far as the Woodbines at that very moment, for they were about to find out that their only son had perished.

Police officers were everywhere and seemed overwhelmed by the cavalcade of cars that sat idling waiting to be shown where to go. Jack didn't have the patience. He steered his vehicle to the end of the bushes, parked and got out. Wearing his FBI jacket, he groped through the frenzy of reporters who were at the ready with their cameras in tow; steadying their microphones for the verbal onslaught.

A soulful wind blustered while Jack galloped up the imposing front steps. The leaves cascaded along his feet with a soft, rustling voice. After reaching the top, he rang the doorbell and heard the chimes bewail his presence. A distinguished man answered the door, asked his name and the reason for his visit. He was let in.

Wow, look at this place. Everything was positioned in its respectable area, like a furniture showroom. The curtains were large and magnificent; they hung from ceiling to floor as the chandelier encompassed the entire hallway. He feasted his eyes on the formal dining room. Its luxuriant hues enriched the ambiance.

"May I take your coat?" the man asked with a charmed English accent. He was dressed in formalwear and looked every bit the butler.

"I'd like to keep it on," Jack requested. "That's if you don't mind?"

"Not at all," the butler replied.

"Should I take off my shoes?"

"That will not be necessary."

Jack nodded. *That's good, because I've got a hole in my left sock.*

"I'll make the governor and his wife aware that you are here, Agent Stanwick." He turned around and ambled away.

Jack admired the hardwood floors. The staircase looked as if it had a hundred steps leading to the second floor with a grand banister he would've slid down on as a kid. Servants were abundant. They were scampering around with what he assumed were their last-minute orders.

The butler walked up. "I will seat you in the library, Agent Stanwick. Please, follow me."

Jack trekked behind him as they came upon a closed room.

The butler opened the door and they entered. "Please, have a seat," he conveyed in his precise and polished tone.

"Thank you." Jack's voice inflected a subtle pretentiousness.

"You're welcome, sir." The butler exhibited an abrupt grandeur. He pivoted on his heel and hastened away.

Jack laughed under his breath as he studied the room. *There must be a thousand books on those shelves.*

He roamed around the expansive area and came up to a giant globe that was suspended on a golden arc. Jack laid his fingers on the sphere and gave it a strong spin. As it frantically traveled, he closed his eyes and slammed his hand down to stop the motion. He checked under his palm and saw it had landed on the island of Tahiti. *I wish I was there instead of here.*

"Hello," a man spoke.

Jack immediately removed his hand and turned around. "Hello." The embarrassment writhed on his face.

The couple walked further into the room. "I'm Governor Jonathan Woodbine." He looked morose in his black suit.

Jack advanced toward them without hesitation and extended his hand.

They met and a firm handshake ensued.

"This is my lovely wife, Hortense," the governor said.

Jack dipped his head in acknowledgement.

She delivered an icy cold glaze.

He took a deep breath. "I'm Special Agent Jack Stanwick with the Federal, I mean..." His nerves had gotten the better of him. "I'm with the FBI." He let loose a strong exhale.

"What makes you so special?" Her eyebrows furrowed.

Is she for real? "It's just a title, ma'am."

Governor Woodbine turned toward a wet bar. "May I offer you something to drink, Agent Stanwick?"

"Ah, nothing for me. I'm on the job."

"Hortense, darling, would you like one?"

"Just a small apricot brandy would be fine," she responded. "I need something to quell my wretched nerves." Her glare shifted toward Jack.

I'd need to guzzle down the whole bottle to quash mine.

The governor brought two drinks over and handed one to his wife.

"We should probably sit down." The First Lady gestured with her manicured hand.

"Yes, please." Governor Woodbine agreed. He placed his full glass atop a coaster on an end table.

Jack turned to sit in a plush chair.

The Woodbines lounged on their lavish sofa and faced him.

"My Captain told you I was coming, didn't he?" Jack's face turned serious.

"Yes, I've spoken with him," Governor Woodbine sipped his drink.

"Can I ask what he said?" Jack needed to know.

"His discussion focused on the FBI and that you were all doing everything within your power to find my missing boy," Governor Woodbine replied.

"Mr. Stanwick," the First Lady voiced. "Are you indeed doing all you can to procure my son?" She continued with her chilly reception.

What a snob! "Mrs. Woodbine, we've done our best."

"So, you have found him," she stated.

Jack's hand tightened into a fist. "We have found your son."

Governor Woodbine's eyes welled up as he hugged his wife. "Did you hear that, Hortense? They've discovered our son!"

"Careful, Jonathan," she squawked. "You will wrinkle my attire."

Jack watched as she struggled to break free.

"Jonathan, take your hands off me," the First Lady snarled. "You are going to break me in half." She broke his grasp.

When the governor came to his senses, he sat up straight. "Agent Stanwick, this is great news. When can we see him?"

Jack's heartbeat quickened. *What am I going to tell them?*

"Agent Stanwick, did you hear me?" Governor Woodbine asked.

"Yeah...I mean, yes, I heard you."

The governor and his wife stared at Jack.

"It's not good news that I came to deliver." His eyes darted downward.

"Then what is it?" the governor asked.

Jack writhed with tension.

"Mr. Stanwick, would you please get to the point?" Mrs. Woodbine was rabid.

He couldn't take it any longer. "You're son, Carlton..." His gaze remained firm. "I'm sorry, he's deceased."

Grave silence came over the room.

"My Carlton..." Governor Woodbine's body shook intensely as rapid tears sprung forth. "Is dead?"

"I'm afraid so," Jack answered.

The governor let out a wail that could've shaken the bones of King Tut. "Oh, my God," he screamed. "My boy, my boy! I'm never going to see my boy again." Governor Woodbine blubbered uncontrollably as his wife sat stoically.

Jack lowered his head. He despised this procedure.

"How did Carlton die?" The governor bawled.

"My son, did he die by his own hands or by another's?" Her face held no grief.

"Some foreign substances were found in his body…"

"Drugs!" Mrs. Woodbine scowled.

"I didn't say that."

"I knew it." Her tone rang abrasive. "He couldn't stay away from that stuff even though he promised me it would cease." She stopped. "Mr. Stanwick, I need to give you some background into our lives. I don't want the press tainting our good name."

"Please, not now, Hortense," Governor Woodbine groaned as he moaned ferociously. "Our son is dead. Have some compassion."

She hurled a look of horror at him. "Compassion is for the weak."

Jack's eyes bugged. *What's wrong with this woman?*

The First Lady continued. "So before I was so rudely interrupted…" Her eyes darted toward her husband then back to Jack. "I wanted to let you know that I was born into a very conservative Virginian family. My father, Jackson Eubanks, was a Governor of this great state and my mother, Grace Stallworth, is the daughter of steel magnate, Weston Stallworth. I have been taught from a young girl that our family is not the type who will air their dirty laundry in public." She spouted forcefully. "We are very well connected here in the South. I practically won my husband the governor's seat."

"Hortense, please…" Governor Woodbine pleaded as he continued to bawl mercilessly. "This man doesn't want to listen to your nostalgia right now. He came to discuss our son."

"He has no choice." Her glare pierced through Jack. "He's in my house and I want him to get the story straight from the horse's mouth before the press taints his view of us. This story will be told."

The governor sniveled. "Yes, dear."

Would somebody start the press conference? Jack sat back knowing she would continue her story.

"I met Jonathan in college as I was in the process of becoming a lawyer." She held her head high. "At that time, he was pursuing a degree in accounting, but when we courted with the mission of marriage, I firmly told him that I would only marry another fellow lawyer. I wanted someone in my league." Her head went even higher. "So, he became an attorney."

"I've heard this story a hundred times, and it's best when rushed along," the governor said. "I was the valedictorian of our class. We were wed then worked together at the same law firm. When I made partner, she wanted me to become the mayor, and then when the governor's position became available, I become the shoe-in and accomplished both in two years. When Hortense became pregnant, she left the law firm and never went back. She now basks in the glory of being the First Lady."

"Jonathan, really," Mrs. Woodbine snapped as she swatted at him. "I was telling the story quite perfectly."

"I know, dear." Jonathan cowered. "I'm sorry. I got carried away."

Her look went from anger to disgust in a second flat.

Jack took command of the room. "We need to discuss this case and what will be said at the forthcoming press conference."

"What am I to say?" Governor Woodbine asked as he began to sob savagely, a pond puddling in his hands. "My son is dead." He violently thrashed. "Why can't I be left alone?"

"Jonathan, stop it!" Hortense scolded.

The governor vehemently shivered. "I need to grieve." He clutched a throw pillow, smashed his face down into it and for the moment doused the intense drama.

Mrs. Woodbine moved away from him and sat in a chair. "I am sorry about the display. My husband is obviously not well."

Jack shook his head. "I understand." He was mesmerized by her behavior. "I'd probably act the same way if my only child was ripped from my arms."

"You probably would." The First Lady touched one earing then the other.

This woman doesn't have a heart.

They heard a bitter cry. "It wasn't suicide, was it?" Governor Woodbine sprawled out to consume the entire couch and vigorously yelped.

"Hush, Jonathan," Hortense said with furor. "And stop that disturbing behavior at once!" She glared at him with intensity. "Pull yourself together. What on earth is this poor agent going to think of you?"

Jack stared at her. *I think he's fine under the circumstances. You're the emotionally-stunted snob.*

The governor stopped wailing. "I'm so sorry," he sniveled.

"Well, that's better." The First Lady glowered. "Now, sit up straight and act like a governor."

Jonathan started to rise up then fell back again. "I can't," he hollered. "My son!" The Governor clutched his heart. "My son, my beautiful son," he wailed repeatedly.

"Bancroft, come here," Hortense yowled.

The butler arrived at once in his professional manner. "Yes, madam, you called?"

"Jonathan, get up," she shrieked. "Go with Bancroft." The command went henceforth.

The Governor slowly sat up and helplessly staggered to the butler, who led him away.

What a difficult life Carlton must have had. No backbone for a father and a tyrannical mother. No wonder he succumbed to drugs. Jack was irritated.

166

"I am livid about that display." The First Lady laid her flattened hand against her perfectly-coiffed hairdo. "Jonathan has never been adequate under pressure. Thank goodness he has me."

There's nothing good about that. Jack's eyes frowned.

"So Mr. Stanwick, what drugs were found in Carlton's system?"

The spotlight was now on him. "Carlton was injected with some chemical compounds." He handed over the brown envelope. "You'll find it all in here."

The First Lady snatched it as repulsion scowled over her face.

Jack edged back. *At least she feels something.*

"I have told him so many times that those stupid drugs would kill him someday." Hortense pulled the contents out. "Well, that day has finally come." She squeezed them.

"They weren't your run-of-the-mill street drugs, Mrs. Woodbine."

She looked up from the crumpled documents. "What about the foreign substances you mentioned previously?"

"The chemical compounds are made from synthetic substances that had been mixed with plants, shrubs and berries from the Amazon rainforest," Jack retorted. "The resulting solution was then injected into your son. They weren't, as I said before, drugs that a person can commonly buy on the street. This elixir was pharmaceutically-hatched and mixed with natural elements. I'm trying to find out for what purpose this was done, but I need your cooperation."

"How?"

"I need to bring the Davenport Detective Agency in on this case.

"Is that really necessary?" she asked with obvious caution. "I don't want to bring on a media circus."

"Mrs. Woodbine, they're very discreet." Jack knew how to work her. "They'll help me to close the case quicker, and that'll stop the press from invading your privacy. That is what you want, isn't it?"

She clutched at the strand of pearls hanging around her neck. "Well, of course I do, but..."

"Mr. Stanwick, bring them in," a masculine voice ordered.

Startled, they swung their heads in the direction of the door.

"Jonathan!" The First Lady dropped the documents onto the floor and stood to her feet.

Jack knelt down and picked them up.

"You're back!" She hurried toward her husband. "Are you feeling better?"

He slowly walked in. "I'm much better."

Mrs. Woodbine took his arm and led him to the sofa. "Here, Jonathan, lay down."

"No, I feel all right." The governor grasped her hand. "Why don't you sit down next to me?"

The First Lady sat down in a poised position and crossed her feet at the ankles.

"Hortense, I'll take over now," he asserted. "Carlton would have wanted me to. I should have taken a firm hand with him a long time ago."

"Yes, Jonathan." An aura of reverence came upon her face and erased the rough edge.

Now that's the spirit! Jack handed the documents to the governor and smiled.

The First Lady looked on.

"Oh, my God!" He gasped as his eyes roved over the photos. "Is that my Carlton?" The governor's voice cracked. "What's wrong with my son?"

Jack quickly intervened. "A kind of metamorphosis took place."

"Why does he look this way?" Governor Woodbine trembled as the tears streamed down his face. "What's happened to his appearance?"

"That's what we're going to find out," came Jack's determined reply.

"Mr. Stanwick, you said that some drugs caused this," the First Lady stated.

"No, not drugs again!" Governor Woodbine roared. "I've told him a thousand times that they'd kill him someday." The howl was bloodcurdling. "Why didn't he listen?"

"As I told your wife earlier, they weren't illegal street drugs," Jack remarked. "It was a combination of rare materials from nature and some formulated drugs made by pharmaceutical companies that were injected into his system."

"How would he have gotten hold of them?" The governor put out his hands. "Did he order them from his computer?"

"I'm not sure." Jack shrugged. "That's why I need help from the Davenport Detective Agency. They have access to channels that I don't; legal loopholes and all."

"Mr. Stanwick, do we really need all these people?" the First Lady questioned. "The less they know the better."

"I understand your concern, Mrs. Woodbine, but they're very discreet. I've worked with them before."

"I don't want the media all stirred up."

"Hortense!" Governor Woodbine bellowed. "I'll take care of this."

169

She immediately sat back.

"I understand my wife's concern." He gently tapped her knee. "The media have skewered my son on multiple occasions, along with our parenting skills." His mood had calmed down. "All I ask is that you and the people you're hiring be discreet with this case moving forward."

"You have my word."

"Good." The governor looked at his wife. "Then it's settled."

"Not quite," Jack countered. "There's one more thing. On paper, it must look as if you hired them on your own. My hands need to be kept clean. I've got the FBI to contend with."

"Yes, you do." Governor Woodbine agreed. "I, on the other hand, do not. Just let me know what you need and I'll personally see that you have it." He stood up. "I appreciate whatever you can do for my family."

His wife rose from the sofa and straightened out her dress. She took her husband's arm.

Jack hopped to his feet.

"Right now, I've got to stay strong. My son needs us." Governor Woodbine reached into the pocket of his pants, retrieved a monogrammed handkerchief and blew his nose.

"Governor..." It was the press secretary. "The conference is set to begin soon."

"Thank you."

"I'll be right next to you on the stage to shield any uncomfortable questions." Jack leaned in. "I've done a few of them."

"Thank you, Mr. Stanwick." Governor Woodbine dipped his head. "I'm extremely grateful for all of your assistance." He extended his hand while the First Lady bared a beleaguered expression.

"You're quite welcome." Jack grasped the hand firmly and shook it. "If there's anything you need, just let me know."

Governor Woodbine nodded his head. "Please, just help my boy's reputation. It's been sullied enough."

"You got it." Jack stepped back and watched as the press secretary briefed the governor. As the rehearsal took form, he walked out of the mansion, up onto the stage and slid into his spot by the podium. The press buzzed about in anticipation and appeared ready for the attack with their stinging questions. After a while, the press secretary came up and stood by him.

"Everything good?" Jack's pose remained impenetrable.

"It went rather smoothly," the press secretary replied. "He's a pro."

Cameras flashed as the governor and his wife stepped onto the stage. They walked by the bodyguards and raised their hands in the air. It looked more like an inaugural win than a death notification. In the spotlight that she craved, the First Lady held a monogrammed handkerchief in her hand. As the crowd grew silent, Governor Woodbine approached the podium, clung onto it, leaned forward and began to speak into the microphone. The news anchors stood readied.

"Ladies and gentlemen of the press, I want to thank you for coming on what is now a day of sorrow. Moments ago, an FBI agent informed the First Lady and me that our son..." He stopped and took a deep breath. "My son, Carlton was found dead."

Horrified gasps came from the stirring crowd. Brouhaha bubbled forth as a flurry of flash bulbs lit up the dreary day.

Mrs. Woodbine cried on cue as the governor put his head down and was obviously in deep pain. An aide rushed up to assist them. Jack overheard Governor Woodbine tell the man that he needed to continue for Carlton's sake.

Governor Woodbine cleared his throat and spoke with clarity and conviction as the clustered mass calmed down.

"The Federal Bureau of Investigation has assured me that they will use everything at their disposal to find out what happened to our son."

"Governor, are you seeking reelection?" a reporter shouted.

"My family needs closure before I debate the issue."

Another reporter hollered. "What about the explosive fight between Carlton and his girlfriend, Amanda Watson?"

"Were alcohol or drugs involved?" another person from the press yelled.

Jack instantly intervened. He cupped his hand around the microphone to ensure that his voice didn't sound over it. "Governor, you don't have to answer any of them."

"I do," he insisted. "My son's reputation is in question."

Jack stepped away.

"According to her statement, they had dinner at Sinclair's. There, a bottle of wine was shared. Afterwards, it was drinks and dancing at the nightclub, Bliss. Supposedly, some alcohol was consumed and a minor argument ensued. She became upset and wanted to leave, but he was adamant on staying. Amanda took his car keys and ordered him to take a taxi home. Carlton never arrived."

The First Lady put her gloved hand on her husband's arm and leaned into his ear. "That's enough, dear."

Jack heard it and watched the governor pull his arm away.

"As far as illicit drugs, we were informed that Carlton had none such in his system."

"Governor, was he kidnapped?" someone yelled.

"I cannot comment on the issue."

"Where was he discovered?" another person screamed.

The crowd pushed against the platform.

"How did he die?"

"Was he murdered?"

Jack jumped toward the microphone and covered it once again by his hand. "Governor, don't answer that."

Governor Woodbine fell against his wife. The press secretary grabbed hold and ushered him off the stage toward the mansion.

"Folks, that's all we know for the moment." Jack took control. "As the case unfolds, we'll keep you posted on the developments. Please respect the privacy of the Woodbines and thank you for coming."

The crowd grumbled and murmured as they dispersed.

Jack ran up to the governor, who was being escorted away.

"Sorry about that." He walked backwards to face him. "Reporters, they're out for blood."

"And guts and glory," Governor Woodbine lamented with his hand to his forehead. "It's all politics."

"Yeah."

"Do me a favor, Agent Stanwick," the governor entreated with a harried voice. "Find out what happened to my precious boy, please!"

"I will."

"Thank you," Governor Woodbine said. The tears burst forth as he was whisked away.

Jack turned and looked at the trampled lawn as crushed leaves blew by his feet. Someone grabbed him from behind and held their hands over his eyes. He clutched the wrists, ducked under them then viewed the person.

"Simone!"

"Hello, Jack!" She smiled. "Did I surprise you?"

"Yeah..." A huge grin came over his face. "But it's a good one."

"The Washington Tribune sent me down for the press conference since I was the one who broke the story."

"I left a message with my partner to tell you about it if you called."

"You did?" She leaned in. "That was sweet."

Jack smirked. "I know."

"Why didn't you just call me?"

"Things have been really crazy," he replied. "Look at the press conference, for instance. It's been a hectic few days."

"I see your point."

"Are you going back to Washington, DC, soon?"

"Why?"

Jack stared at the ground. "I was just wondering if you wanted to stay for a while and maybe..." He hesitated.

"What're you proposing, Mr. Stanwick?"

"How about I take you to dinner?"

Her eyes sparkled. "I thought you'd never ask."

Jack grinned.

"What about your case?"

"I have three guys—no, make that four, who're helping me with it. One night of relaxation, albeit on the FBI's dime, isn't a big deal. Nobody will be the wiser."

Simone looked up at his face. "I will be the wiser." She smiled.

"Well, guess I stand corrected!"

"Speaking of corrected, I've already written my article for tomorrow's edition and there are a few lines that have to be reedited. I'll send it on with Dave, my cameraman. He's leaning against the car over there." She pointed her finger.

Jack looked over then back at her. "How did you get it done so fast?"

"Well..." Simone paused. "I wrote it earlier."

"But the press conference just ended." A befuddled look fell over his face. "What, your story doesn't mention Carlton's death?"

"It does," she replied. "I knew he was dead. When Buford called and told me, I knew."

"What, Buford called you?" His eyes squinted. "Why didn't you tell me?"

"For the same reason you didn't tell me about the press conference."

"And what would've happened if his death wasn't announced today?"

"I would not have run it."

He glared at her. "Oh, you wouldn't have..."

"I promise you!" Simone put her hand over her heart. "It wouldn't have been in this edition."

Jack took a deep breath and looked away. "Okay."

"Let me go and tell Dave I'm riding home with you."

"Wait, I'm spending the night."

Simone stopped. "You are?"

"If you stay in town tonight, we can experience the night life of Virginia."

"I'd have to find somewhere to spend the night."

"I'm staying at the Bonaventure Hotel," Jack remarked. "They might have a room available?"

"And if they don't."

"You can sleep in my bed and I'll order up a cot."

Her face beamed. "Sure, why not," Simone stated. "Let me give Dave my draft. I need to give him some instructions."

"Super, I need to make a call anyhow." He pulled out his cell phone.

She ran off.

"Hello."

"Is Raymond in? It's Jack Stanwick."

"Sure, one moment, please."

"Hello, Jack!"

"Hi, Raymond, do the guys have any news for me?"

"Hold on, I'll put them on speaker phone."

Anxiously, Jack asked, "Guys, are you there?"

"Yes," Bren replied.

"What've you found?" Jack inquired.

"I've discovered..."

"Like, we've discovered, dude."

"Yes, Russ," Bren bellowed. "I meant we've discovered two chemical plants within a two hundred mile radius that'd be capable of producing pesticides."

"I jumped on my computer and found several Buford Higgins in the area," Derek stated. "I correlated them and found one lives within seven miles of a plant called Prescott Chemicals. From there, I hacked into a couple of home security systems that this man might use and voila, he was registered with Syntac Home Systems. I took his information and passed it on to Bren.

"So I called Prescott Chemicals and asked if Buford Higgins was there. The secretary replied that he was. I informed her that the alarm at his house was tripped and it was sending an alert to his home security system. She told me to hold on while she checked to see if he was in the lab. I waited until a man with a slight drawl came on the line. I asked if this was the Buford Higgins that lived on Grimes Road a few miles from the chemical plant. When he replied it was, I again stated that the alarm at his home had alerted us and that an officer was dispatched. I further instructed him to go to his residence and see what has transpired. He thanked me and hung up the phone."

"I wish we totally had enough evidence to go and take that dude down," Russ blurted out.

Jack intervened. "We don't want to spook him," he remarked. "Buford has to go back to his normal routine while we collect the needed ammunition."

"Yeah, we need to catch him off-guard," Derek noted.

"We need a solid case with irrefutable proof," Jack claimed. "I need to know if he's indeed the one committing these heinous acts and if there's somebody helping him. Most of all, where's this concoction being made and stored?"

"We have a plan," Bren replied. "Since we know that Buford Higgins is employed at Prescott Chemicals, we'll go there tonight and see what we can uncover."

"Yeah, we're taking the Camaro with the duped plates just in case we're seen," Derek stated.

"Like, there's no catching us dudes," Russ quipped.

"You won't get caught," Jack added. "You guys know what you're doing."

"That's true!" Derek belted out.

"We figure everybody should be gone except for the cleaning crew," Bren related. "The three of us will sneak into Prescott Chemicals. We'll find out if they are indeed producing this deadly mixture."

"You guys know you're breaking and entering," Jack issued.

"They know," Raymond said.

"Well, since I can't talk you three into not going, at least see what's going on there. Call me if anything pans out."

"We will," Bren declared.

"Thanks, guys!" Jack hurried. "I need to tend to something so I'll talk with you soon."

Simone was heading his way.

He shut off his cell phone and slid it into his jacket pocket.

"I hope everything went well."

"It did." He smiled. "Are you ready to go to the Bonaventure Hotel?"

"First, I need to do some shopping," she replied. "I've nothing to wear. Plus a girl needs her toiletries, especially if she has to make a presentation in the morning."

Jack put his arm out. "Then shopping it is."

Simone slid her arm through his. "That's the best comment I've heard all day."

A sly grin appeared. "No comment!"

They both snuggled up to each other and walked arm and arm to his car.

Chapter 12

Simone exited the elevator and entered the lobby of the Bonaventure Hotel. Exquisite paintings lined the pastel yellow walls as an embroidered trim elegantly weaved along the borders. Sconces were placed to add soft lighting to an already warm setting. They had agreed to meet there.

Jack walked up and gave her a long-stemmed red rose. "I was in the gift shop looking for some mints and this lovely creature caught my eye."

"It's beautiful!" Simone accepted it with a delicate hand.

"Speaking of beautiful..."

"This hotel certainly is."

Jack grinned. "The company isn't half-bad either."

Simone smiled. "I'll take that as a compliment." She brushed his shoulders. "You're looking quite dapper yourself."

"I'm glad we found that men's shop." He nodded. "It's surprising what a new pair of pants, shirt, tie and blazer will do for a guy."

"I wasn't referring to your clothes." She winked.

"How's your room?" He changed the subject.

"It's fabulous and large, almost the size of my entire apartment."

"Then you should see the size of mine." He stopped. "I mean my house."

"I knew what you meant."

Jack turned his flushed face in the direction of the hotel restaurant. "Do you want to eat here or would you rather see what else is in the area?"

"I'd rather walk around and take in the sights. I noticed some cute cafés as I drove to the press conference."

"That's fine with me." Jack put out his arm. "Shall we take that leisurely stroll?"

"Sounds simply divine." She took his arm.

They departed the Bonaventure Hotel and went out onto the street. Wafts of crisp air stroked their faces as they lingered along the busy walkway. Jazz music filtered out the open doors of the local fare while shoppers loitered in front of the assorted boutiques engaged in rapt conversation.

"The city is quite busy," Simone commented.

"It's hopping tonight." Jack nuzzled closer to her.

She didn't beg off.

"People love to eat out, don't they?" Simone asked.

"Well, it is Friday night," Jack replied. "Most are cooped up all week with work. They can finally go out and let their hair down."

"Is that what we're doing?"

He touched the graying at his temple. "I don't have much to let down."

"I've enough for the both of us."

"That you do." He pushed a lock behind her ear.

Simone winced. "I'm so ticklish." She giggled.

"That's good to know." He sported a roguish grin.

"No, it's not!" The words lingered from her lips.

Jack dropped the subject. "Do you want to stop in one of these places?" He pointed at a clothing store.

"No, thank you," Simon replied. "I did enough shopping this afternoon to last me at least…"

"A year?"

"A week!" She swatted his arm. "What kind of woman would wait a year?"

"A financially frugal one."

"Those words aren't even in my vocabulary."

Jack felt her let go of his arm and watched her form a regal stance.

"Do you like the dress I bought today?"

"Very much!" His eyebrows raised. "It perfectly caresses all your nooks and crannies." *Nooks and crannies…where did that come from?* "I mean it looks better on you than the mannequin."

She laughed and clung onto his arm. "Nook and crannies—that's a first!"

"Yeah, for me too." They resumed strolling.

"Where should we eat?" he asked. "I mean, is there a type of food you fancy?"

"When I drove through here today, I noticed a cute little eatery a couple of blocks away," she replied. "Would you care to dine there?"

"Just lead the way."

They walked a couple of blocks and happened upon a fanciful French bistro named Sage.

Simone stopped. "This is the place."

Jack glanced inside the open door then nodded with approval. "Good choice."

"I just adore French food," she said in her best French accent.

"It's been a long time since I've had French food."

"I just love it, but it can be quite the heavy meal."

"Then eat it with a light fork."

"You've just got all the answers."

"You just ask good questions."

She gave him a hearty smirk as they entered the restaurant.

"Wow, it smells so good in here!"

"Yes, it does."

"I'm so hungry, my stomach is growling." Jack rubbed his abs. "I'm ordering everything on the right side of the menu."

"I'm hungry myself," Simone added. "I'll take everything on the left."

"It'll probably plow through the majority of my 401K."

A paunchy man in a tuxedo approached them. "A table for two?" he asked with a strong French accent.

"That'd be great," Jack replied.

"Right this way, please."

Jack leaned into Simone as they walked. "He must be the maître d'."

"I can see why you're a detective."

They were escorted to the other side of the restaurant to a cozy spot in the corner. One elegant candle softly burned in the middle of the table.

"I hope this will be satisfactory for you?" the maître d' asked.

"Very satisfactory," Jack uttered.

"I'll send your waiter right over." The maître d' turned around and left.

Jack pulled out Simone's chair in a manner befitting a gentleman.

"Why, thank you, sir," she said with a slight southern accent. "Chivalry is not dead."

"No, little lady, it's still alive and kicking," Jack touted as he pulled out his own chair and sat down.

Laughter burst forth.

"I feel he thinks we're a couple," Simone said.

"Now looks who's being the detective."

"I'm just saying it's secluded, yet romantic."

He donned a frisky grin. "It is, isn't it?"

Her face glowed amidst the candlelight.

"This place is crowded tonight." She turned her head.

"Yeah, it's a very busy place," he added. "They must have good food."

The waiter approached their table. "Bonjour, my name is Gaston. Here are your menus." He handed them out. "Would you care for something from the bar?"

Simone smiled. "I would love a glass of white zinfandel, please."

"I'll take a chardonnay." Jack hoped it would help him to unwind. "Could you also bring us two waters with lemon, please?"

"Yes," the waiter replied. "I'll be back momentarily with your drinks."

Simone looked at Jack. "You remembered I like lemons."

"I remember everything."

"Of course, you're a detective."

Jack nodded.

"I see you're a wine drinker."

"Honestly, I hardly drink at all, but it'll relax me tonight."

"Are you nervous?"

"Yeah, about the case."

"Anything in particular you want to talk about?"

"No," he muttered. "You being a journalist and all."

"I'm also a concerned citizen," she said in a huff. "And by the way, I clocked out a few hours ago."

"I should too."

"Yes, or it'll make you a boring dinner companion."

"A glass of wine should get the ball rolling."

"I hope in the right direction."

"I just need to relax and not be constantly thinking about work all night," he said. "I wish sometimes my brain could be shut off with a switch. The way one turns off a light. Work tends to be on my mind every waking moment."

"I know exactly what you're saying. When I've got a deadline, look out."

"Try having a case to solve."

"No, thanks. My work is crazy enough."

"Yeah, it's difficult sometimes to separate business from pleasure," Jack admitted. "But tonight, it's going to be pleasure."

"Yes, definitely pleasure." Simone agreed. "No more talking about shop. I don't want to be a boring date."

"A date, huh?"

"It's a play on words. I guess I should say—a word."

"Oh." Jack looked wounded.

"But a date isn't out of the question."

The waiter arrived and put the wine in front of them along with a basket of baked bread. Jack immediately grabbed his glass and took a healthy gulp.

"Thank you." Simone picked up her drink.

Jack nodded his head. "Yeah, thanks."

"I need to fetch your water with lemon," the waiter said. "In the meantime, do you want to hear our specials?"

"Please," Simone replied.

"First, there's Coq au Vin, which originated in Auvergne. It's fresh, marinated chicken cooked in a white wine sauce with pearl onions, portabella mushrooms and a soft bouquet of garlic."

Jack winked at Simone while they both sipped their wine.

"Next, we have Steak Maurice. It's tenderloin of beef that's been brined, sliced thin, grilled quickly and served in a garlic wine sauce with soft blackened potatoes and our vegetable du jour."

Jack's eyes perked up as he thought about that tasty morsel. He was about to order it, but the waiter kept on.

"And last, but not least, is the Salmon Coullbiac. That dish is fresh salmon wrapped in a crepe, stuffed with a spinach mousse, baked into a pastry puff and served with our famous dill beurre-blanc sauce."

They both placed their drinks down and looked at the waiter.

"I'll give you a moment to decide." He turned around and left.

Simone glanced at Jack. "I'm going to have a hard time selecting a meal."

"It all sounded so good. Maybe we can order one of each and share."

"This dress is too tight to share."

He laughed and she joined in.

After taking a sip of wine, Simone asked, "Have you decided on what you're getting?"

Jack shrugged. "What about you?"

"I might order the Salmon Coullbiac."

"I'm leaning toward the Steak Maurice."

"That also sounds delicious. It's hard to make a decision."

Jack drank some wine and watched Simone do the same. He didn't want to head back into the rough territory he previous ventured through so he steered the conversation in a different direction. "So tell me a bit about yourself?"

"What do you want to know?"

"Oh, let's see." Jack's eyes shifted about. "When you were born, where you grew up, do you have a boyfriend, why you became a journalist, are you married, what's your shoe size?"

Simone sat upright. "I enjoyed your attempt at being humorous, yet personal, all at the same time."

"Almost didn't get that all out."

Her sculpted eyebrows curved. "Well, let me see, I was born in Syracuse, New York at St. Joseph's hospital in the latter half of the 1970s. The very late half." Simone smiled. "I grew up about twenty miles west in a little town named Baldwinsville. While I was growing up, I'd love to interview the neighborhood kids to find out about their lives. I also enjoyed playing detective games. My friends and I created different scenarios and put clues around designated areas and someone would have to

186

solve the crime. I loved it when it was my turn, so I could figure it out. I always did. What fun we had."

She paused, picked up her wine and sipped it.

Jack did the same.

"In high school, I became the reporter of our school's newsletter. I'd cover local events in the community such as baseball, basketball and football games, our pep rallies or whatever was newsworthy. One time, I actually investigated what I thought was a case, but it was actually some of my friends playing a major joke on me. The things we did when we were kids. Oh, well. From there, I graduated high school and went to Syracuse University for journalism and creative writing. I became a journalist because I wanted to emulate Barbara Walters. I'm not married; I don't even have a boyfriend, and my shoe size is a seven, just in case you see a pair of Jimmy Choo shoes."

"Jimmy who?" Jack asked.

"Never mind," Simone replied. She drank the last of her wine.

The waiter came up. "Have you decided what you're having for dinner?"

Jack nodded then looked at Simone.

"I'll have the Salmon Coullbiac, please," she replied.

"Excellent choice," the waiter said. "What kind of dressing would you like on your salad?"

"A low-fat honey mustard, please."

The waiter turned to Jack. "What may I get you, sir?"

"I'll have the Steak Maurice and ranch dressing on my salad."

"An excellent choice as well, sir," the waiter said. He collected the menus. "Would you both enjoy another glass of wine?"

Jack piped up. "Yeah, we would."

"Did you want an appetizer with your wine?"

Jack glanced at Simone.

"No, thank you," she replied. "I couldn't eat all of that."

The waiter smiled and walked away.

Jack felt good from the wine and started to unwind. "So you don't have a boyfriend."

Simone's eyes widened. "Not currently," she uttered. "What about you?"

"No, I definitely don't have a boyfriend," he quipped.

She giggled.

"Nor do I have a girlfriend."

"When was the last time you were in a relationship?"

"Forever ago," he reacted. "And you?"

"I dated a fellow journalist from the Washington Chronicle. His name was Tim. That lasted about two years. He wanted to get married, but all I desired was a career first, and him second. I needed my independence and was so afraid a husband would hinder my goals. I wanted to fly out at a moment's notice for any story. It seemed the more stories I covered, the more our relationship suffered. Not to mention we were in competition for the same assignments. There was a discussion about him taking a position at another newspaper, but it never came to fruition."

"Working and living together must be hard."

"It is! The two of us argued over headlines and bylines, and our views turned critical of each other's stories. We fought more than we cuddled when watching television. The only passion we had was for our own careers. At the end, it became such a nightmare that we decided to part ways. After turning in my resignation, I went to work for the Washington Tribune. It's now time for me to slow down and smell the roses." Simone picked up the long-stemmed beauty that Jack got her and put it to her nose. "It smells wonderful. Thanks again."

"You're welcome again." A grin encompassed his face.

The waiter brought more wine to the table. "Your meals will be out shortly."

"Thanks." Jack nodded.

The waiter exited.

He lifted his drink and took a sip.

Jack watched Simone raise the wineglass to her lips. He relaxed further.

"So Mr. Stanwick, tell me about yourself."

"Well, let's see. I was born in 1972 and raised near Bethesda, Maryland. Being an only child was pretty cool. Every summer since I can remember I spent at my grandparent's house on Chesapeake Bay. It was so much fun."

"I bet it was beautiful."

"It was." He took another sip of wine.

"What did you do as a child?"

I also liked to play detective. Cops and robbers was another game I'd play with my friends, except during the summer. Then I'd be a private investigator because there were no other kids to hang out with. I had to entertain myself. It's pretty much older people who lived on the island." Jack picked up his wine glass and snagged another gulp.

Simone did as well.

"Every morning, I'd go down to the bay to see what washed up overnight. There might have been a case that needed solving. I always hoped that a bottle would wash upon the shore with a note in it from someone who was stranded on a desolate island somewhere out in the Atlantic Ocean. I'd save them, get my name in the newspaper and become a big hero. Such a crazy idea, right? Just the dramatic mind of a bored little boy."

"All children fantasize," she stated. "I did."

"Just wanted to help people, I guess." He fiddled with his fork on the table. "I used to assist the old lady that lived next door to my grandparents by carrying her groceries home every week. She'd give me a dollar. I thought it was all the money in the world. I'd buy a package of bubble gum and a soda pop every time. After I drank it, I'd rinse it out in the ocean, let it dry a couple of days then put a note in it saying, 'My name is Jack and I live on Chesapeake Bay during the summer and whoever gets this note, please write me back!' After I'd done that a couple of times, my grandpa caught me and told me it was littering so I never did it again. I never got a note in my bottle back either."

"That is so sad."

"It wasn't a big deal." He shifted in his chair. "The sad came ten years later when a drunk driver killed my grandparents and mother as they pulled out of a supermarket parking lot."

"Oh, Jack." Simone's eyes moistened.

"Even sadder, my dad worked around the clock so he didn't have to come home. He eventually moved into the Chesapeake Bay house and I stayed living in the family home. Between his law firm and my work, we hardly ever saw one another."

"I am so sorry." A couple of stray tears rolled down her cheeks.

"I didn't mean for it to make you unhappy."

"It's the wine." She sniffled. "Sometimes it makes me so emotional."

He handed over his dinner napkin.

"I have one, but thank you."

Jack watched as Simone brought the napkin up to her eyes, dab them a few times then put it away. She picked up her purse, pulled out a circular item and looked into it.

"I'm such a mess!"

"No you're not."

Simone reached back in, took a colorful bag out and rummaged through it. Once the item was retrieved, she ran a line under each eye then returned it.

"Is everything all right?"

"My eyeliner melted off so I had to fix it." Simone dropped her purse to the floor. "Damage control is done!"

Jack grinned. "Good."

She picked up her glass of wine. "So you were saying…"

"Well, I went from the bay to the police academy and worked there for eleven years before applying to the FBI."

"What brought about that decision?"

"To advance my career," he replied. "I wanted more control and bigger assignments. Definitely got what I wished for."

"Have you worked on any high-profile cases?"

"You sound like a reporter."

"Ever the journalist, even when I don't mean to be."

Jack leaned in. "I helped solve the Horoscope Hitter and the Black River serial killer cases."

"I wrote about them. They were awful."

"So is this current case. I wish I had more to go on."

"It'll all come to fruition. I have faith in you."

Jack balked. "That makes one of us."

"You must have a partner. Don't most FBI agents work in pairs?"

"Yeah, I've been with Blaine close to seven years."

"What a handsome name."

"Blaine would think so." Jack smirked. "He'd say it matched his looks."

"He can't be as good-looking as you."

"Of course not!" His shoulders broadened.

The waiter brought their entrees to the table and systematically laid them down. "Would you enjoy another glass of wine?"

Jack looked at Simone.

"One more, please, and then I'm done," she said. "I don't want to stagger back to the hotel."

"Make that two, please. We'll stagger back together."

The waiter retrieved the glasses and walked away.

Jack watched Simone as she took a couple of bites of her meal.

He picked up a forkful and sent it down the hatch.

She put her fork down, picked up her napkin and dabbed both sides of her mouth. "Do you know of a Harvey Welch?"

Jack began coughing as tiny bits of food flew into his hand. He wiped them with the napkin then took a gulp of his wine."

"Did you get some food lodged in your throat?"

"Yeah, something like that..." His voice cracked. "Why did you ask me about this Harvey Welch?"

"Buford Higgins had sent me a letter telling me to look into the man's history, so I did."

"What did you find out about this guy?"

"Not much," Simone replied. "He was supposedly a hit man with the notorious Carmini family a few years ago, but went into hiding. Now he's found murdered at the same Granite's Mill where Carlton Woodbine was discovered." She She shrugged and picked up her fork. "I wonder what was going on with them two."

"Beats me!" Jack snatched his fork and shoveled some food into his mouth.

Simone picked up her glass. "What was the toughest assignment you've worked on?" She sipped the wine.

"It had to be the Giarrosso case." Jack took a bite of his food.

"Why?"

"In many ways, it changed how we handle kidnappings at the FBI."

"I'm not familiar with that case. What happened?"

"I was a rookie agent and shadowed the case." Jack leaned forward. "These two guys kidnapped a seven-year-old named Will Giarrosso. The family was extremely wealthy, you know...old money. The kidnappers wanted one million dollars and told the family not to contact the cops or their son would be killed. The money drop was issued and the wait began."

"Giarrosso—wasn't he the former mayor of Chicago?"

"Yeah, one and the same."

"That's the time period when I went to my parent's house and stayed awhile to get away from my break-up with Tim, the man I told you about earlier," Simone said. "I started with the Washington Tribune after it all happened, but I did read bits and pieces when I found the newspaper which my mom and dad seemed to always be reading. We only got the Sunday edition."

Jack nodded. "To make a long story short, after the kidnappers received the money, the Giarrosso family waited for the return of their son. Two days went by, but no child appeared. The cops were finally called in...then the FBI. We checked street and ATM cameras, telephone calls, voice recognition modalities, fingerprints, DNA samples, even eyewitnesses from the child's neighborhood and school in case the kidnappers had cased it." His face eased. "That information led us to one of the suspects..."

The waiter placed their glasses of wine in front of them. "How is your meal?"

"Delicious," Simone replied.

"May I get you anything else?"

"No, we're fine," Jack answered.

The waiter left as they both sipped their wine. Jack appreciated that Simone listened intently. He noticed how stunning she looked and how she kept up her end of their conversation intellectually. He took another bite of his food.

She lifted her fork. "So what happened next?"

"This suspect chirped like a bird," he retorted. "The sad part was the young boy was killed, supposedly by the other suspect. This same guy then went and murdered the parents to tie up any loose ends. The perpetrator figured there wouldn't be a conviction due to the lack of evidence. He thought wrong, and was later killed in a shootout."

"How could somebody do such a thing?"

"I don't know." His head hung low. "I was bothered by that case for months."

"How did the FBI change the way they handled future kidnapping cases?" she asked.

"They've warned people in the media that the first twenty-four hours are the most crucial and how the police have to be involved immediately. The FBI use hostage negotiators and trained officers in the matter of kidnappings. Canine units are also used in the pursuit. These tactics have been very helpful."

The waiter came to the table to remove the dishes. "May I get you anything else? Perhaps some dessert?"

"No, thank you," Simone responded. "I need to watch my girlish figure."

"I've got to watch it too." Jack grinned.

Heads tilted back in laughter.

"Here is the check." The waiter laid it close to Jack.

Simone reached over.

Jack intercepted. "I've got this." He grabbed the check and pulled out his wallet.

"Remember, I pay this one. I told you that at lunch yesterday."

"If I'm remembering it correctly, you'll be picking up the tab when I give you the entire interview about the case."

"Well, that game plan has changed." She edged in and snatched the check.

The waiter bent down and whispered. "Sir, never argue with a woman."

"I can see that!" Jack shoved the wallet back into his pocket.

Simone handed over her credit card. "I just love plastic, especially with bonus points."

The waiter walked off then promptly returned with the receipt. "Here you go, Miss. Please sign the top copy and keep the second for your records."

Simone filled it out and handed it back.

"Thank you for dining with us." The waiter turned and walked away.

Jack swigged back his remaining wine. "Are you ready?"

"In a moment." Simone leaned forward. "I wanted to say something, but I know you didn't want to talk shop. I feel this information is too important to sit on."

"What is it?"

"Buford called and told me there was a fifth body that was actually the first victim a couple of years back. He instructed me to look for the son of a powerful man then hung up." She kept her voice low. "I looked up all the males who died over the last few years in Washington, DC and Virginia, but nothing stood out. Do you know anything about this?"

Is she playing me? "No." He shrugged. "Maybe it's a con or a set up."

"I had such a rapport with him," she stated. "Maybe somebody walked in on the conversation and he had to get off the phone, because he called me Arvin and said something about meeting later. I thought that a little strange."

"That's what a con man does, and this one has a crush on you," he added. "That can be a dangerous combination."

"With that bit of information, I'm now ready to go!" She lifted her purse off the floor and rose up.

Jack stood from his chair.

Simone faltered when she took her first step.

"Whoa, easy does it." He grabbed her arm and slid it into his. "There you go."

"I'm sorry, Jack," she said. "I'm a little lightheaded."

He grinned, a little unsteady himself. "Well, hang on tight."

They exited the restaurant and leisurely strolled back to the hotel. Once there, Jack summoned the elevator. They got on and the doors closed.

"Thank you for such a lovely evening." She leaned against him.

"You paid." Jack held her tight. "But you're still welcome."

The elevator stopped.

"I guess we're home." Simone got off.

"Guess so." Jack followed her up the hall.

They stopped at her hotel door. She rummaged around in her purse then pulled out her keycard. He took it from her hand and opened the door. Simone walked in and turned around. Jack felt awkward, so he looked into her eyes hoping for a sign.

"Well, goodnight." She leaned in and kissed him on the cheek.

Startled, Jack uttered, "Goodnight, sleep tight. Don't let the bed bugs bite."

Simone winked. "I won't let them."

His face reddened. "That's a jingle my mother used to say to me every night when she tucked me into bed."

"It's quite cute." She smiled, closing the door.

Why did I just say that? Jack stood there and thwacked his hand against his forehead. *That was so stupid!* He heard the lock unlatch then the door opened.

"What are you doing?"

"Um..."

Simone grabbed Jack by the front of his shirt. She yanked him hard with a firm hand, raised him off his feet and planted him in her room. The door swiftly slammed shut.

Chapter 13

The detectives drove down I-95, exited the off ramp in Cantor County and traveled west for roughly forty miles into the vast darkness. With map in hand, Bren slowed down and turned right onto a country road. He maneuvered along the winding curves until Prescott Chemicals came into view.

"There it is!" Derek pointed.

Bren veered off Whiskey Hollow Road and continued toward the steel structure as the moonlight shimmered off a mammoth chain-link fence surrounding the entire complex. They passed the unmanned guard post and drove by the open gate. After fifty or so feet, he turned the car around, parked next to a wooded area and shut off the lights. The engine was next.

"Like, I cannot believe we found this rank place," Russ quipped.

"We would've been here sooner if we had a GPS on this Camaro," Bren groused. "At least our Lexus has one."

"I printed out MapQuest to find our way here." Derek held it up. "Who knew there'd be all these little roads sending us into the boonies?"

Bren smirked. "That's the reason I always bring my atlas on a road trip."

"Let's not forget we took this car because it has bogus plates registered to a John Smith—the most common first and last name in America—that way it cannot be traced back to us,"

Derek stated. "Not to mention I have it buried so deep in the DMV database that even the Geek Squad couldn't resurrect it."

"Like, speaking of dead, this place is majorly on the slab," Russ uttered.

"What did you expect?" Bren sneered. "A parade to announce our arrival!"

Derek intervened. "Let's just move and groove."

They all got out.

"Whew, this place sure smells nasty!" Derek recoiled.

Russ grabbed his nose. "Like mad nasty."

"It's a chemical plant." Bren snarled. "It should have an awful odor."

Derek rolled his eyes at Russ as they kept pace along the fence.

"It sure is quiet out here," Bren commented.

Russ peeked over his own shoulder. "This place is totally dark and creepy."

"Yeah, it's a bit eerie," Derek added.

Bren scowled. "Just concentrate on our task at hand."

Once reaching the open gate, they stopped to scope out their surroundings.

"I see four cars on the side of the building," Derek spoke.

Russ snickered. "Like, it's totally the cleaning crew."

"Then they are the highest paid ones on the planet." Bren's finger pointed. "The first one is a Mercedes C class, the next is a '69 Camaro, the third is a Lincoln Continental and the last is a '57 Thunderbird."

Derek and Russ stared at him.

"What?" Bren croaked.

"For a guy who was born with a silver spoon in his mouth, it shocks me that you'd know the year of two classic cars," Derek remarked. "Especially in this dimly lit parking lot."

"Do you guys remember I told you about my uncle Garrison, who was a police officer killed in the line of duty?" A dismal look covered Bren's face. "When I was a young boy, he had a mint classic T-bird of the same year. Every once in a while, we'd wash and wax it and then go out for a drive." His eyes dropped. "When his will was read, the car was left to me, but I couldn't look at it, nor would I have driven it. My dad knew, and sold the vehicle. The money was given to me and I donated it to the Boston Police Foundation. Little did I know I'd become a police officer eight years later."

"I didn't know I was going to be a police officer either," Derek added.

Russ smirked. "I totally did."

Derek gritted his teeth.

"Like, I didn't know either."

Derek smiled while nodding.

Bren looked up. "I know what the both of you are doing." His head turned. "I'm not that fragile." He scoffed. "Let's take this building apart!"

"I hear you." Derek agreed. "Guns locked and loaded?"

"Totally," Russ replied.

The detectives strode across the parking lot. They arrived at the steps and marched up to the top. Bren grabbed the front door and it opened. "That was easy enough." He motioned for the guys to enter.

There was silence everywhere.

"Like, nobody's around," Russ uttered.

"Somebody's here," Bren said. "The front doors were unlocked."

"If we get stopped, you're Buford Higgins nephew," Derek remarked. "Say we just got into town and swung by to see if your uncle was still here."

Bren nodded. "And we're here to take him for a late dinner."

"That sounds majorly cool." Russ grinned.

"Now keep your eyes open and your mouths shut." Bren walked on.

They went down the hallway and came to the elevators.

"We can't take this," Bren noted. "It will make too much noise."

The detectives walked further.

"Look, there's a stairway," Derek commented. "That'll be quiet enough."

Bren sneered. "Only if Russ doesn't gallop down them."

"Like, I don't gallop," he said. "I've got a totally cool swagger."

Bren rolled his eyes. "Then get swaggering."

Russ opened the door and headed down the flight of stairs, followed by Derek and Bren. After reaching the bottom of the grated steps, they crept down a corridor.

"Russ, you're sneakers are squeaking," Bren hissed. "Pick up your feet."

"I am, dude," he murmured.

"Shush, guys!" Derek used a hushed tone. "It is nerve-racking enough without you two fighting."

"We're not fighting," Bren whispered. "We're discussing."

"Well, discuss another time," Derek muttered.

They arrived at a closed door. Bren slowly opened it and looked around the area. "The coast is clear."

Derek entered and Russ followed. They walked and came upon some huge equipment. Everything hummed with action. The lights were on. Somebody was there.

"This area seems to have been newly constructed," Bren said.

"Wow, it's so clean for being a chemical plant," Derek commented. "I thought it would be very dirty in here."

"Like, it's spic and span," Russ uttered. He observed the various gadgets and gizmos that were displayed on the machinery. "Look at these totally cool things twirling and whirling about."

Bren leaned in. "These instruments are reading temperature, pressure, and flow rates." He looked to the side and touched the panel. "That's a chromatograph. It isolates different compounds and their reactions to specific chemicals."

"And it's attached to a computer," Derek noted. "Now this is my specialty."

Like, duel nerds. Russ grinned.

Derek tapped a button. "There we go."

"Should you be totally messing with it?"

He faced Russ. "If I can hack into governmental databases without getting caught then I can certainly hew into this." His fingers moved across the keyboard.

"Like, your fast, dude."

"I'm in." Derek looked at the screen. "It's quantitative analysis."

"What is that?" Bren edged in.

"The data on chemical compounds," Derek replied. "Basically, it's readings on volatility, precipitation, extraction, distillation and so on. A scientist can graph these percentages to obtain the exact measurements of a mixture. The preparation would have the most advantageous results—the perfect formula."

"Like, I wonder what stank stuff is being made."

"Who knows?" Bren shrugged. "We need to keep walking."

"I thought he knew everything," Derek whispered to Russ.

"So, not even close."

As they continued down the hall, Bren stopped. "I hear voices."

They listened.

"I hear them too." Derek nodded.

"Like, they're totally up ahead." Russ bypassed Bren and took the lead.

"We need to stay quiet," Derek urged.

They crept further back to where the voices were coming from. Although the talk was spirited, Russ couldn't make out what they were saying and from the looks on their faces, the others could not either.

"We need to get closer to hear the conversation," Bren whispered.

"How?" Derek asked. "There's nothing to hide behind."

Russ scanned the area. "Like, take a gander up there." He pointed above his head. "There's a majorly humongous pipe right there, and look…" His finger moved to another location. "There's a mad ladder on that vat. We can totally climb it, grab the pipe and hoist ourselves up."

Derek smirked. "Then what, swing from it like a flying trapeze?"

"By the volume of their voices, there's no drop ceiling on that room," Bren noted.

"We'll just scurry across it, sit totally on the elbow and way listen in on their conversation," Russ suggested. "Like, the darkness will keep us way hidden."

"You're joking, right?" Derek looked up. "I won't be doing any scurrying. It can't be more than twelve inches in diameter, and it's got to be around five feet above that nine-foot unit. That's close to fourteen feet off the ground."

"Do you see any alternative?" Bren posed.

"But I'm afraid of heights," Derek whined. "It's darn near pitch-black up there."

Russ shook his head. "Stop being a total wuss!"

"You need to deal with it," Bren insisted. "Remember the Barrington case when we had to cross the beam on that construction site?"

Derek grimaced. "Yeah, all too well."

"That was much higher off the ground," Bren held. "You made it, didn't you?"

"Obviously!"

"Dudes, let's totally do this." Russ headed toward the ladder. He led them up the rungs then across the pipe. "Like, look in that vat." His head sloped. "There's some grody fluid in it."

"Never mind," Bren hissed. "Derek, don't look down."

"Don't worry..." His voice shook. "I won't."

The detectives climbed the ladder, balanced across the pipe as if on a high wire and stopped at an elbow that hung over the room. Four men were engaged in a discussion. The detectives crouched down and eavesdropped.

"Listen, Arvin! I don't care about the Christian Coalition riding your back. If you cannot manage being the president of M.A.G.O.C., then hand it over to someone who will. Henry Prescott is up for the challenge."

"That's the Speaker of the House, Logan Price," Bren whispered. "I recognize his voice from a press junket he did a while back."

"I can handle my position over M.A.G.O.C.," Arvin ranted. "Remember, I'm the damn founder of the militia organization. You just need to take care of your end of the bargain."

"I will!" Logan snapped. "I'm just waiting for somebody to get the formula right. As soon as that happens, I'll enact the plan."

It'll be ready for another trial run within forty-eight hours," Buford claimed.

"You told us that everything was formulated and ready for implementation last week," Logan groused. "Instead of getting the elixir right, there's three guys taking up residence in the FBI morgue."

"At that point, I had yet tested it on a human, but it is getting better with each body," Buford cited. "You try taking a native's concoction that changes a lad into a lady with one sip and see what you can do with it. I'm just taking extra precautions to ensure the natural component is not degrading or being diluted with all the additional synthetic materials I've added."

"And what if that happens?" Logan questioned.

"The formula would be rendered useless, but that won't happen," he answered. "I've been using the compounds quite cautiously. I want the formula to produce the best results."

"That's Buford Higgins," Bren said. "I recognize his voice from our previous phone call."

Derek hardly moved, but Russ scanned him.

"Like, you're totally two for two."

"I need that formula to alter the masculine brain into a feminine mind. Females are more emotional than males. They relish sentimental love where males like the physical presence,"

Logan droned on. "Also, women think with their hearts, where men think with their guts. They're the weaker vessel and need to be taken care of. You know the old adage in the Bible at Genesis that states, 'The woman will crave the man and he will dominate her'..."

"Those words hold true today," Henry spoke up.

"A woman will do anything for a man and to keep a man," Logan added. "The old 'I'm pregnant' trick traps a man all the time."

Arvin jumped in. "Who did you get pregnant?"

"Not me!" Logan crowed. "I'm too smart for that stupidity."

"Women are conniving," Buford noted. "You'd better watch out for this Lydia person because she might have an agenda."

"She does," Logan stated. "It's to take care of me and to assist you on the formula."

"I'd be mighty careful with an educated one," Henry remarked. "Women need to be willfully controlled."

"Not all of them are willing," Arvin declared. "Some are spewing that equal rights crap."

"Well, even with those feminist broads hollering, they're still seventy cents to our dollar." Logan smirked. "Women need to realize it's a man's world, and to stop their presidential jargon. They should be grateful we've elected a couple to the Supreme Court. Lord knows Congress has enough of them."

"By the way, what measures are kicking around the old Capitol Building?" Henry asked.

"There's a new gun control amendment making the rounds that'll take all automatic weapons off the streets and put them in the hands of the police," Logan answered. "The Democrats have already pushed gay rights and their ability to marry through the Supreme Court by way of the new justices, which the president hand-picked..."

"I bet that hasn't boded well with the bible-thumpers," Buford piped up.

"There's also steam picking up about the immigration issue," Logan continued. "Pretty soon, they'll steamroll right over our Constitution with pregnant women, drug cartels and Spanglish."

"The Christian Coalition should go ballistic over those issues," Henry expressed. "I hope fellow Republicans are listening to the NRA and battling hard against any and all new gun bills."

"I don't understand why they want automatic weapons off the streets." Arvin shrugged. "It's mostly minorities that are killing themselves off. Who should care? The immigration issue would take care of itself."

"It'll clean our cities up without the government lifting a finger," Buford added. "There'll be less welfare trash sucking the system dry. It'll save food stamps, public assistance and our Medicaid program for those of us that'll need it someday. It's a win/win situation all the way around."

"Now we just have to rid ourselves of the gays," Arvin uttered. "The government should grow another AIDS virus, and this time, make it ten times stronger. It should be able to drop one dead gay a day…"

"And threaten the lobbyists of their pharmaceutical companies that they'll be ejected from their pocketed constituents if they make any drugs to counteract the virus," Buford blurted out.

"There should be one for the geriatric population too." Arvin continued. "Just let it loose at some nursing homes and various retirement communities and poof! There go the oldsters up in smoke like a cremation."

The detectives look at each other. Their appalled expressions said everything.

"Logan, you told me there's more legislation when I talked with you before," Henry stated.

"I wasn't finished!" He rattled off with an attitude. "With Mutt and Jeff hijacking the conversation, I couldn't get a word in edgewise."

Henry glared at Arvin and Buford. "Go ahead, Logan. The floor is yours."

"There is talk about some kind of treaty with the Arab Emirates. They want peace and security. Good luck. That won't happen. Not with North Korea wanting to exert their measly power or Russia with their plans on world domination. Then there's China who could outbid them both with their hidden nuclear weapons. "

"What about the oil?" Henry enquired.

"There's been a call on members of Congress to phase it out, along with natural gas," Logan reacted. "Instead, they will substitute them with water, solar, wind and geothermal power; with the building of nuclear reactors as the cornerstone in hopes of stimulating the economy. Oh, and get this. The Democrats are fully against hydro- fracking. They're such fools!"

"I've got major stock in oil and natural gas," Henry griped.

"We all have them," Buford groaned.

Arvin shook his head. "Not me."

"That's because you're an idiot," Logan quipped.

Arvin chuckled. "Well, who's the idiot now with all those soon-to-be useless stocks?"

Buford snickered. "Certainly not the loser prize-fighter."

"Shut your damn mouth!" Arvin balled up his hand. "Do you want to end up like Harvey?"

Buford folded his arms. "You just try it!"

Arvin jumped at him as Henry blocked his body. "Stop this nonsense, both of you," he shouted. "What's the problem?"

"We need to work together," Logan replied.

Arvin dropped his threatening gesture and stepped back. "Sorry, Bu. All this news has made me jumpy."

"Me too," he muttered. "Sorry."

"That's much better." Henry patted both their shoulders. "We're all brothers here."

"It's this damn formula," Buford grumbled. "I can't seem to perfect it."

"That's why we're bringing in Lydia Reome to assist on TB4711," Logan stated. "That'll take some pressure off you and onto her."

Buford nodded. "Okay."

"It'll all work out, you'll see," Logan assured.

"Speaking of working out," Henry spoke. "Why not make Harvey Welch the scapegoat?"

The men looked at one another. "Yes!" Logan sneered. "But how?"

"We could leave some clues at Harvey's place?" Buford suggested.

Logan grinned. "This is sounding better by the minute."

"I'll do you even one better," Buford boasted. "I have the kid's jacket up in the lab."

"What kid?" Henry asked. "The governor's son..."

"Wait, the rich leather one you had gotten rid of?" Arvin interrupted.

"Yeah, I thought I did."

"You lying sack of crap," Arvin growled. "You wanted it for yourself." He balled up his hand. "I oughta knock your block off!"

Henry put his hand over Arvin's fist. "There will be no knocking of blocks today."

"Do you have any solution that could be placed at Harvey's place?" Logan asked.

"Yeah," Buford replied. "But it'd look better if the cops found a vile of it in the kid's jacket pocket. That would create even more suspicious activity."

"I like the way you think." Logan nodded. "I have a set of Harvey's house keys and I will plant them there. The police have already scoured his house so I'll call in an anonymous tip before getting back to Washington, DC."

"Phew!" Henry exclaimed. "I'm glad this problem was solved."

"We have another one," Buford mentioned. "I'll need test victims to see how the formula is progressing. Any of you want to volunteer?"

"Hell no!" Arvin retorted. "We'll just do our usual drive around late at night and find us some targets." He puffed. "If Henry was willing to let me bury the mistakes way back on his many acres, I could scatter the bodies all over the place."

"Sure, that way the FBI, CIA or whatever other initials are investigating won't find any more corpses," Buford remarked.

"No...not...never!" He roared louder with each word.

Arvin shook his head. "Why not?"

"When are you gonna get it through that bruised, battered, beaten-down head of yours to let it go?" His voice rumbled. "Your old boxing days must've killed too many brain cells."

"Whoa, no hitting below the belt!" Buford uttered.

"Guys, let's first bring Lydia on to formulate the solution to the exact proportions before any more bodies are discovered anywhere," Logan said. "Can we at least agree on that?"

All nodded.

Bren, Derek and Russ looked at one another, wide-eyed.

"Is there anything more going on in the White House we should know about?" Henry asked.

"The Dems have been talking about later terms on abortions and the cloning of organs with embryonic stem cells," Logan responded. "They're also adamant on taxing religion while legalizing illicit drugs to lower the massive debt ceiling. I've also heard rumors that our government now has the capability to listen in on cell phone conversations under the guise of terrorism. It won't be long before the militia groups are in their line of fire."

"Then we have to act fast!" Arvin croaked.

"That's why we need Lydia's help," Logan remarked. "I'm bringing her to the Back Alley Bar tomorrow night to meet Henry. Hopefully, everything will go according to plan."

"I can't make it," Arvin mentioned. "I'm holding the M.A.G.O.C. meeting to inform the members about what's going down."

"Who invited you to come?" Logan asked. "Just kidding!" He stepped aside. "Don't bite off my head."

"I'd feel better ripping it off and handing it to you," Arvin snarled.

"Let's simmer down, gentlemen," Henry declared. "Buford won't be there either. He'll be making room for Lydia in the lab.

"Well, I'm glad we had this little chat," Logan stated. "I need to get back to Washington and get some paperwork done before Lydia arrives."

"We'll walk you out." Henry turned his head. "Buford, make sure you turn off the lights."

A cell phone rang.

"It's mine." Logan pulled it out of his suit coat's inner pocket. "Hello." There was a pause. "What?" His eyes widened. "Are you sure?" He looked panicked. "Okay, I got it," he squawked. "I said I've got it!"

"That sounded serious!" Henry looked concerned.

"The local police are setting up road blocks on either side of your chemical plant!" Logan's hand shook as he put the cell phone back into his pocket. "The FBI is on its way with warrants. I can't be seen here. This will devastate our plan, and I won't survive in prison." He wrung his hands. "What should I do? What shall I say?"

"First you need to get a grip," Henry advised, turning aside. "Buford, run to the lab and make sure everything is buckled down. Take Arvin with you then meet me at the car. Now, hurry," he barked. "And don't forget the kid's jacket with the formula in its pocket."

Both dashed away.

"As for you, you're getting out of here. There's a way. As for me, I have a button to push!" Henry scuttled Logan down the hall.

Moments later, everything became dark.

"Like, they're gone," Russ uttered.

"Thank God," Bren stated. "I know of four men that will be going to hell, and probably with a French woman in tow."

"I can't believe what we just heard!" Derek remarked.

"I wished they would've mentioned who the poison was for," Bren said.

"Like, those dudes are totally mad," Russ quipped. "We so need to find that grody concoction and majorly destroy it."

"Yes, and soon, before they use it again on some unsuspecting soul," Bren added.

"My legs are totally cramping." Russ stood up. "Like, they need some major blood flow."

"Mine are numb," Derek declared. "I've got to stand."

"You need to go first," Bren posed. "We can't bypass you."

Derek raised his body and began to slowly slide one foot then the other. "I can hardly see. My eyes have barely adjusted to the dark."

"Be careful." Bren followed him. "You're not exactly wearing the best shoes for walking across a pipe."

"No, they're better for hiking or kicking some butt." Derek inched forward.

"That's why I totally wear Converse sneaks," Russ stated. "Like, they've got major gripping power."

Derek flailed his arms.

"Are you okay?" Bren asked.

"I can't see that well."

"Then go slow."

"I'm losing my..." Derek fell to the side.

The others heard a splash.

Russ looked down, lost his balance and started slipping. He grabbed Bren's arm as they flew off into the solution.

All splashed around vigorously as they choked, gasped, and panted before Derek jumped to his feet.

"Guys, stand up," he shrieked.

Russ surged upward and yelped. "Like, oh my God!"

"I'm soaking wet," Bren screamed as he surfaced.

"What the hell is this stuff?" Derek asked.

"Who knows?" Bren retorted.

"I've totally lost my gun!" Russ felt around frantically in the solution to find it.

"My brand new Ralph Lauren jacket is ruined," Bren bleated. "It cost me over nine hundred dollars."

"Shut up, dude!" Russ sloshed around in the liquid as he continued to search. "We way don't need your whining."

"Just take it off," Derek suggested.

"I am. Besides, it's too heavy being wet with this crap." Bren removed it. "It has such an odor anyways."

"I totally found it!" Russ lifted up his revolver.

"Good," Derek expressed.

"Like, it'll probably seize from this stuff." Russ aimed it.

"Don't touch the trigger," Bren bellowed. "This crap will probably blow us to smithereens."

"Yeah," Derek yelped. "They will be finding little charcoaled pieces of us all over Virginia."

"Just put it back in your pants," Bren spouted.

"Slide it in your band," Derek added. "I tuck mine in the back of my Levi's."

"I angle it in front, just inside my briefs so it doesn't fall out," Bren inserted. "It stays secure."

"Like, it's so slimy, dudes, and you want me to slip it in my boxers?"

"It wouldn't be the first time that something slimy was in them," Bren retorted.

"At least mine gets way slimed," Russ uttered. "This is the only time yours will be totally wet."

Bren gave him a dirty look.

"Okay, guys…" Derek intervened. "Enough!"

A large grinding noise took them by surprise as the floor began to move.

"What the hell?" Derek yelped.

Russ jutted out his finger. "Like, there's another ladder in here."

Water came gushing out of an overhead shaft dousing them.

"Hurry, before we are sucked down into purgatory," Bren roared.

Derek jumped on and hustled up the rungs. "They're slippery so watch out."

"Russ, hurry up," Bren squawked. "Your rear is in my face."

"Shut up before I totally kick your rank stank back in."

"Go ahead," Bren rumbled. "I'll take you down with me."

"C'mon guys, knock it off!" Derek climbed down the other side.

Russ reached the top, slung his body over and started down the ladder.

"How do you enjoy my rear in your face?" Bren asked. "I can still totally yank you off," Russ replied.

"You guys, cut it out!" Derek groused.

Russ grumbled. "Like, dude way started it." He leaped off the ladder and Bren followed.

"Just let it go." Derek begged. "We got to get out of here."

Russ stood frozen.

"What're you doing?" Bren asked.

"Duh, we've got to find that grody formula," Russ replied.

Derek shrugged. "We have no clue where it's hidden."

"We can't do that tonight," Bren said. "We don't know what this solution is that we fell into. Let alone where the formula is. We'll come back another time. I need to take a shower to get this off of me."

"It's been on our skin long enough," Derek remarked.

Russ frowned and pushed his shoulder-length locks back. "This totally wretched stank might be wreaking havoc on my curls."

"That rat's nest you call hair is all you ever worry about," Bren stated. "I swear you must have Munchairsen by Peroxyide."

"Huh?" Russ' face rumpled.

"It's supposed to be Munchausen by Proxy," Derek replied.

"Like, whatever!" Russ snapped. "You want me to totally rip that rug off your head?"

"Mine is natural, you fool," Bren retorted. "I happen to like my hair perfectly combed into place. It is certainly better than looking like a stoner who had just crawled out of the bushes at a Jimi Hendrix concert."

"Stop it, guys," Derek declared. "We need to get a hotel room and wash this stuff off before our bodies absorb it."

"He's right," Bren added. "We have to go."

"Like, totally." Russ agreed.

They headed down the hall and dashed up the steps. Derek reached the top first and fumbled for the door handle.

Bren snarled. "Open it already."

"I'm trying to, but it's dark in here," Derek stated. "Wait, I found it."

"Let's so blow this popsicle stand," Russ quipped.

Once the door opened, Derek ran and the other two followed. When the detectives reached the main entranceway, Bren immediately stopped.

"Look, they're still in the parking lot." He pointed.

Two men were standing near a car with their backs to the detectives. There was one person in the driver's seat. He had the door partially open and was facing in their direction.

"Arvin's sitting while Henry and Buford are standing," Bren noted. "I don't see Logan anywhere."

"We need to run to the car with all our might," Derek uttered.

Russ peeked over his shoulder. "Like, they'll totally see us."

"Not if you keep your backside to them," Bren stated.

"Just haul butt," Derek remarked.

"Is everybody ready?" Bren asked.

"Let's totally hit this," Russ blurted out. He flung open the doors and barreled out as Derek and Bren raced behind him.

"Look over there," Arvin shouted. He stood up from the driver's seat. "Three guys are gunning across the parking lot. Let's get them!"

"Don't bother!" Henry raised his hand to stop him. "It's only the Williamson boys. I chase them out of here all the time."

"They think this place is their personal playground," Buford clamored. "I've got half a mind to bring in my shotgun and fill their backsides with some lead."

Henry raised his other hand to stop him. "They're not hurting anything."

Buford stepped aside. "If you say so."

"I say so!" Henry settled.

Buford shook his head. "Why're we just standing around like sitting ducks?"

"If we run, the authorities will think we've got something to hide." Henry rationalized. "And I for one am clean as a whistle."

"So are we," Arvin declared.

Buford snickered. "I don't know why you had Logan drive out back on Dead Creek Road, as you named it, so he could get away?"

"Look at it this way," Henry answered. "If Logan was caught here with us, wouldn't that look mighty suspicious, him being the Secretary of State up in Washington, DC? What on God's green earth would be an appropriate excuse for him to use?"

"That he was lost," Buford retorted.

"And what or whom was he visiting?" Henry sneered. "His great aunt Bessie?"

"Maybe..." Buford concurred. "I mean it is possible."

"Now you know why I'm a leader and you two are followers," Henry remarked. "When the establishment pulls in, I want the both of you to keep your mouths shut and your ears open. Got it?"

Neither of them said a word.

"That's exactly what I want to hear—nothing," Henry growled through gritted teeth. "Maybe, just maybe..." His fist shook at Arvin and Buford. "I'll be able to spend the night alone in my fifteen by twenty-five foot bedroom instead of an eight by ten cell with you two fools!"

Chapter 14

The detectives rounded the corner of the open gate, rushed toward the car and jumped in. Bren started the engine and threw the gearshift into drive. He slammed his foot on the gas pedal and burned rubber.

From the passenger seat, Derek rolled the window down as Russ howled out from the back, "Yee ha!"

Bren sped along the dusty road and swerved to miss the empty guard post. He exited onto the darkened country road and raced away from Prescott Chemicals.

Russ watched out the back window. "Like, I think we're clear."

"I'm glad we made it out of there alive!" Derek leaned back.

Bren eased off the gas pedal. "I second that motion."

"That totally makes three."

Their cell phones rang in the glove compartment.

"Where's the latch for this damn thing?" Derek fumbled around.

The overhead light came on. "Like, that should make it way easier."

"Not to mention it's your car," Bren declared.

Derek jerked it open and yanked out the clamoring cell phones. He hit the speaker button while simultaneously shutting off the other ones. "Hello."

"Where are you boys?" Raymond inhaled.

"About five miles from Prescott Chemicals!"

Raymond exhaled. "I've been calling your phones for over an hour."

"What's up?" Bren asked.

"Jack and several FBI agents are on their way to Prescott Chemicals with search warrants, and arrests are inevitable," Raymond replied. "I wanted to give you boys a heads-up."

"That's awesome!" Derek raised his hand backwards.

Russ thwacked it with a high five. "Way awesome!"

"Yes, it is." Raymond agreed. "Between the evidence gathered by us, Jack and Simone, a judge signed them on the spot."

"After what we heard tonight, probable cause would've gotten them a signature," Bren touted.

"Like, three of the four culprits were still outside the place when we beat feet out of there," Russ uttered.

"That's good news, because the local police should now have roadblocks on either side of Prescott Chemicals," Raymond chimed in.

Derek pointed. "Here come some headlights." Several cars and vans zoomed past them.

"Whoa, those dudes are totally on a mission," Russ quipped.

"I see flashing lights up ahead!" Bren speeded up.

"I will come upstairs to talk with you boys in the morning," Raymond mentioned. "I will get the particulars then."

"We're probably not going to be there," Derek noted.

"Like, we fell into some lame liquid and now smell majorly rank," Russ added.

"You guys should get a hotel close by," Raymond suggested. "That way you can shower and sleep there. Just stop in and see me when you get home."

"Sounds like a plan," Derek stated. "We'll catch you later." With that, he hung up his cell phone.

Bren stopped a few feet ahead of the roadblock as an officer waved his hands. He rolled down the window.

A policeman approached. He shined a flashlight on each of them. "So where are you boys coming from all sopping wet?"

"Officer, is Special Agent Jack Stanwick around?" Bren asked.

"Hey, Burwell, tell that FBI agent that he's got a couple of youngsters asking for him."

Moments later, Jack stepped out of the crowd and hurried toward the detectives.

"Thanks, Officer Hopkins. I'll take it from here." Jack leaned his head into the driver's side window.

"You look worse for wear!" Bren sniffed. "I also smell the fruit of the vine."

Derek piped up. "Someone's also been roughhousing, if you know what I mean?"

"Like, for sure," Russ blurted out. "I've had way too many of those nights."

Jack ignored their wisecracks. "Why're you guys drenched?"

"Let's just say we wrestled with a tank of fluid and it won," Derek retorted.

"Did it happen at Prescott Chemicals?" "Totally!"

"What kind of fluid?" Jack probed. "Was it the formula?"

Bren grimaced. "I hope not!"

"Besides, the floor opened up as another liquid came pouring down on top of us," Derek remarked.

"Like, if it was that wretched formula, it's down the floor and out the door," Russ uttered.

"It tasted like salt water," Bren noted.

A surprised look came over Jack's face. "You got some in your mouth?"

"Everything passed our lips," Derek responded.

Russ snickered. "It's a total shock we didn't drown or go majorly down the drain."

"I'm glad you guys are in one piece," Jack declared. "I just wish we could've gotten a sample before it was liquidated."

"We do," Bren countered. "I have some plastic laboratory cups in my duffle bag. As soon as this shirt comes off, I'll wring the solution out and into the sealable container."

Jack jolted his fist. "That's great!" He placed a hand on the roof and leaned back in. "Anything else you might've overheard?"

"Oh, yes," Bren responded. "Those men are quite close to perfecting that elixir they've injected into the three known bodies," he related. "They want to use it on somebody. We just don't know who."

"And they're just sitting in the parking lot shooting the breeze as if nothing is going on," Derek spoke up. "But they know something is about to go down."

Russ snickered. "Like, they're just lollygagging."

"Who's at Prescott Chemicals?" Jack asked.

Bren answered this one. "There is Henry Prescott, Buford Higgins and some guy named Arvin. He's the president of a militia group called M.A.G.O.C. Do you know of them?"

223

"Yeah, the acronym stands for: Men Against Government Overtaking Control," Jack replied. "Several of our agencies have been keeping watch over them. There are over a thousand known militia groups that are fairly low key. Mostly they target practice, complain about our president and drink a lot. Majority of them are harmless. M.A.G.O.C. was fairly low on our radar, but this bit of information will shoot them to the top of our watch list."

"Those dudes back there should be totally shot," Russ added.

"Since there's no trace of the formula now, they are thinking we haven't got anything on them," Jack stated. "But a few days in the tombs with around the clock grilling will yield something. Mark my words..." He grinned. "One of them will take a deal. With the death penalty hanging over one's head, all I'll have to do is ask each of them what they want for their last meal."

Russ sniggered. "Like, one of them will so snap, crackle and pop!"

Jack nodded. "I'm hopping so."

"At least you've already got Logan Price," Derek mentioned. "He'll throw all of them under the bus to save his job at the school yard."

"The Secretary of State?" Jack appeared puzzled. "Is he still there?"

"No," Bren replied. "He must've gotten through the blockade."

"Not on my watch!" Jack held a radio to his mouth. "Gibson, has anybody tried to breech your barricade?

"No, not mine," he answered. "It's so quiet out this way that you can hear the darn bugs chirruping."

"Thanks." Jack lowered his radio. "Now what does the Secretary of State have to do with an old formula and the death of the Governor of Virginia's son?"

"Maybe it's payback for something on the political front," Bren suggested. "Or something happened behind the scenes of his personal life."

"I'll pull him up on my computer at home to see what I can dig up from my resources," Derek commented.

Jack looked sideways. "Should I ask what that will entail?"

"If need be." Derek shrugged. "Let's pretend first I can get into the Secretary of State's private, personal or professional phone calls or email accounts."

"Let's pretend that the CIA, FBI or Cybercrimes can find out who hacked into them," Jack countered.

"Okay, let's pretend one could route it through hundreds, if not thousands of IP addresses in minutes that would take those agencies days, weeks or even a year to find out that it originated from the Secretary of State's own business computer in the first place," Derek counteracted. "It's knowing how not to get caught on the World Wide Web!"

"Well, I'm glad it's all hypothetical." Jack winked.

Derek winked back. "Yeah, that's what it is."

Bren smirked. "You two are too much!"

"Hey..." Derek snapped his fingers. "When those goons were leaving, Logan complained about being caught on the premises." He faced the other two detectives. "Didn't Henry tell him 'you're getting out of here, there's a way?'"

"Yes," Bren declared. "Those were his exact words."

Russ nodded. "Like, I so remember that."

"Officer Hopkins, could you come over here?" Jack gestured then leaned into the detective's car. "We'll get to the bottom of this."

"What do you need, Agent Stanwick?"

"Would you ask the local cops if there's a side road anywhere?" Jack requested. "Also, if you could bring me a map of this area, you'd be doing me a huge favor."

"Sure." The officer stepped away.

"Jack, I've got an atlas." Bren hung it out of the window. "It wasn't easy finding this place."

"Officer Hopkins…"

He turned around.

"I don't need a map, but I do need a local cop, and preferably one who knows this area well," Jack noted.

The officer turned around and entered the crowd.

Jack opened the map, placed it on the roof of the car and smoothed it out. He pulled out his flashlight as one of the local cops approached him.

"Are ya looking for a side road, sir?"

"Yeah, do you know where one is?"

"I've lived in these parts all my life and never seen one," the young cop replied. "The only thing nearby that I know of is down yonder Whiskey Hollow Road about two miles. It's a dirt path called Gunnery Trail. It leads to ole' Widow Gunther's house. But I'd be weary of her though. She's an ornery old gator with an even more ornery shotgun."

"Well, thank you for that bit of information." Jack folded up the atlas and handed it back to Bren. "I'll take that under advisement."

"The young cop nodded then scurried away.

Jack raised his radio. "Agent Carter, its Agent Stanwick."

Static resonated. "What do you need?" "Are the three men separated?"

"Yes, and the team is going through the building."

"Do me a favor and ask each man in custody if there's a side exit besides Gunnery Hill off Whiskey Hollow Road."

"I'll get back to you soon."

"Jack..."

"Yeah." He popped his head in the open window.

"Just so you know, they're also bringing a woman on board to help Buford with the formula," Derek continued. "Her name is Lydia Reome and she's some kind of physicist. I'll also look her up when I get home."

"Also those dudes totally hate women." Russ stared out the windshield. "Like, speaking of women..."

Jacked turned his head. "What're you doing here?"

"And a hello to you too," the woman responded.

"I didn't mean it that way," he stated. "I'm just surprised to see you here."

"Now that's somewhat better."

"This can be quite dangerous..."

"So is meeting a source," she interrupted. "Most of them are not the salt of the earth."

"No, they're the scum of the earth."

She nodded. "I rest my case."

"Then come meet the detectives who're helping me with my case." Jack placed a hand on her back as they both leaned in. "The guy in the driver's seat is Bren, Derek has the passenger side and the blonde in the back is Russ."

"Hello, I am Simone Wellington."

"You write the column for the Washington Tribune!" Bren gushed. "I read you every morning."

"Like, usually on the john in our bathroom," Russ blurted out.

Bren's face flushed. "Don't listen to him." He squirmed. "I'm usually at the dining room table." His eyes glared in the rearview mirror.

"I'm sure you guys want to get out of here and dry yourselves off," Jack remarked.

"That would be totally gnarly," Russ spouted.

"Sounds good to me," Derek added.

Bren smiled. "Let us know how things turn out."

"You bet!" Jack nodded.

Simone stepped back. "It was nice meeting you."

"And guys..." Jack jumped in. "I couldn't have done this without your help, so thanks!"

Russ grinned. "Like, all in a day's work."

"And a wet night!" Derek jested.

"Hold on a moment..." Jack held up a finger. "Officer Hopkins, would you wave this car through?"

"Yes, just have them drive slowly toward me."

Jack looked toward the detectives.

"I'll keep it at a snail's pace," Bren remarked.

Jack chuckled. "I'll talk with you guys tomorrow."

The window went up as the car crept toward the barricade.

"Agent Stanwick, its Agent Carter."

"Go ahead."

"Just one will talk, and it has to be with a Simone Wellington. Is she present?"

"I'll get back to you." Jack lowered the radio as he looked to her. "Buford will only talk with you. How did he know you were here?"

"He called and told me there was something big going down at Prescott Chemicals and that I should be here to write about it."

Jack snickered. "You mean to tell me that you were willing to come out here to no man's land to write about something that might or might not be happening..." He huffed. "Are you crazy?" A scowl appeared. "He could've sexually assaulted you, or worse."

"You don't have to tell me what could happen to a woman," Simone stated. "I am a woman and have thought of them all."

"So why risk your life over something you can't even write about until I give you the word?"

"Because I knew for sure your little sting operation was taking place and I wanted to watch it for myself. One day, when I can write about it, there'll be good reportable data for a series of columns. It's sort of my job!"

"I know you go on dangerous assignments," he said. "I just have to get used to our paths crossing during business obligations."

"And our lanes intersecting during pleasurable allegiances."

Jack grinned as Simone smiled.

"By the way, who told you about our preemptive strategy?"

"A source."

"How would a source know about our closed-ranked meetings?"

"If she's one of the closed-ranked individuals..."

"So you're friends with Victoria Bellows."

Simone's face blanched. "How did you know that?"

229

"Because she owes me a few favors too," Jack retorted.

"Do not say anything to her about this!" Simone urged. "I don't want her to get in trouble for this or sanctioned in any way. She's my old college roommate, and a good friend. I was the only one allowed to call her Vicki."

Jack's expression eased. "I'm not going to say anything."

"Thank you!" She breathed out. "Both of us try to meet weekly so we can have dinner and a good conversation, and we don't talk about work. That's taken off the table so now you can relax."

"That's good news."

"When Buford called to tell me about the meeting here, I'm the one who rang up Vicki. I gave her the information, and she was to say that an anonymous tip had just been called in. I'm sure that's how you found out about it."

"True, but I already knew the detectives were coming down here to investigate and I wanted the proper warrants just in case something went down. That's why I left your room earlier instead of staying."

"I thought it was because I had tired you out."

Jack raised an eyebrow then his radio. "There's a button on the left for talking, so push it in and speak. Let it go when you need to listen."

She nodded as he brought it to his lips.

"Agent Carter, would you put Buford Higgins on the radio?"

"He's sitting in the back of my vehicle right next to me, handcuffed like a pretzel, Agent Stanwick. The others can't hear or see him. Go ahead."

Jack handed it off.

"Hello, is this Buford?"

"Um...yeah, I'm here."

"What did you need to discuss with me?" Simone questioned.

"I'm hearing that the FBI wants to know where the Secretary of State Logan Price had disappeared to," Buford answered.

"Yes they do, but most importantly I want to know where he is," she added.

Jack gave Simone a thumbs-up.

"As long as you want to know."

"Of course I do," she stated. "I enjoy everything you have told me."

Jack scribbled on a notepad then shoved it in front of Simone's eyes.

She nodded. "Buford, did Logan Price drive down Whiskey Hollow Road?"

"To ole' Widow Gunther's place?"

Jack bobbed his head up and down while his hand frantically gestured.

"Ah...yes, toward that way!"

"He'd be a fool to go anywhere on her property," Buford cackled. "Ole' Widow Gunther would fill Logan plum full of holes. Even the mailman won't go to her house. He leaves her mail by a big rock at the end of the trail. She's a pistol, that one."

"I'm sorry I bothered you." The luster left Simone's voice.

"No, you're not bothering me. I'll answer whatever you ask."

Simone took her fingers off both buttons then looked to Jack. "Sometimes it's better to use a woman's soft ingenuity than a man's rough genius."

He nodded.

She pushed the left button. "Did Logan Price escape or is he still at Prescott Chemicals?"

"He's certainly not here," Buford responded.

"So you're telling me he escaped."

"Yep."

"How?"

"Is FBI Special Agent Jack Stanwick right beside you, Ms. Wellington?" Buford asked.

Simone looked at Jack as he took the radio out of her hand.

"I am," Jack answered.

"If I give you this information, will it help me get off the death penalty charge and put on life with the possibility of parole?"

"It depends on what you give me."

"I'll tell you how Logan escaped," Buford stated.

"I'm not promising anything, but a federal prosecutor will certainly look more favorable on a cooperating suspect than one with no information to bargain with," Jack countered.

"Logan Price drove into the back woods and onto an old dirt path that Henry Prescott name Dead Creek Road," Buford told. "It comes out at an old run-down KOA camp that his wife used to own on Hickory Trail."

Jack turned toward some cops and motioned for them to come over. He leaned in and whispered the information he just received.

"Are you there, FBI man?"

"I was writing down the information," he replied. "But I'm afraid you'll have to do better than that."

"How about telling you who killed Vince Graves, and where the body is hidden?" Buford mentioned.

"Vice-President Graves' son?"

"One and the same!"

"No, Vince was backpacking across Europe two years ago when he fell to his death in Switzerland," Jack countered. "We've already wrapped up that case."

"The one where he and this local kid were rock-climbing when the VP's son accidently slipped off an unstable crag when his foot gave way; never to be found?"

"Vince plunged into the rough terrain below which we were told was unnavigable," Jack revealed. "That's why he was never recovered."

"It's malarkey!" Buford crowed. "That local kid, Johan, was paid ten thousand dollars to tell that story knowing nobody would ever find the body."

"So where's Vince?"

"The boy's buried on American soil."

"I take it that he's the fifth body," Jack probed.

"You're a smart agent. No wonder old Gordon Weaver has you on his payroll."

"Are there any more victims we should know about?"

"Not so fast, Agent Stanwick. Not even Simone Wellington would be given this bit of information. At least not without some type of reciprocation," Buford chuckled.

I guess she wasn't playing me after all. "She will be no part of any deal, so go reciprocate yourself," Jack barked.

Buford huffed. "I want a deal from Attorney General Marlene Steele. I don't want to hear she's agreeable to my stipulations. I need everything written down because sorry to say, I don't trust any branches of our government's words. It better be down on paper with a federal seal and notarized by both parties. It needs to read that I will be acquitted of all charges for all crimes past or present, known or unknown, and double jeopardy is to be attached."

Jack cringed. "I don't know if she would go for that, let alone the higher-ups."

"We'll see," Buford stated. "Once Ms. Wellington prints this news in her column, they'll be clamoring for justice. If she listens to your bad advice and doesn't print it, I'll tell it to that girl, um...her name slips my mind, ah...yes, Andrea Edwards at the Washington Chronicle." He sniggered. "Choose your poison well, Simone!"

"Is there anything else I should know about?" Jack butted in.

"Yeah, I'm now bored with you two," Buford grumbled. "Agent, get this walkie-talkie out of my face."

A car door slammed.

"I hope you got what you needed, Agent Stanwick. I'll let him cool down in the backseat for a while."

"Thanks, Agent Carter. I'll be there shortly to get Buford hot under the collar once again. He's close to letting off some steam."

"See you then."

The radio was shut off.

"I need to get over to Prescott Chemicals to keep an eye on things," Jack issued. "There's nothing more going on here that doesn't involve danger. I'd feel better knowing you're safely home. I'll call you tomorrow."

"I want to hear all the dirt!" Simone smiled.

Jack grinned. "It'll probably be mud by the time we're done."

Both laughed as they embraced.

Chapter 15

Once Bren made it through the crowd, he drove for a while until the Interstate Inn came into view.

"Home sweet home," Derek chirped, looking out the window.

Bren huffed. "Why do I have a gnawing feeling this place will be in squalor?"

"We don't have to stop here," Derek responded. "There should be better places to stay the closer we get to I-95."

"Like, no way," Russ blurted out. "This rank stuff we totally fell into could be killing us."

"He's right," Bren remarked. "And that never happens."

"And my hair totally looking this grody never happens."

"Please, that bale of hay on your head could use some moisture," Bren snarled. "Between the glop of products and the constant blow-drying, you're 'waging war on hair-or.'"

"Dude, shut your hole and majorly drive toward that hole." Russ pointed to the bedraggled building.

Bren pulled into the rutted parking lot and stopped in view of the front desk. A partially blinking vacancy sign hung askew in the window. It was more apt to ward off customers than bring them in.

"Like, I so know what kind of motel this totally is," Russ reacted.

"I'm sure you do!" Bren got out. He went in, rented a room and came back to the car. "It's the honeymoon suite!"

"So, it's the last unit on the end," Derek belted out. "Please, tell me there's two beds in the room."

"It's definitely your night."

With headlights off, Bren guided the car to the room. "Here we are!"

A tarnished number 12 clung to the peeling paint on the motel door. Once unlocked, they scurried into the room as Derek scrambled to turn on a light. It reeked of cheap sexual encounters that happened nightly and were paid by the hour. The carpet was stained from one side to the other, while a chipped mirror dangled over a dresser with missing drawers. One lamp without a shade cast a shadow on an already bleak situation.

"Yuck! I can't believe we're showering in this disgusting place," Bren remarked. "Let alone sleeping here."

Derek tossed his duffle bag on a bed. "We don't have much of a choice."

Russ peeked under the beds. "Like, I don't see any roaches or other creepy crawlers."

Derek snickered. "That's because they only lurk around when the light is off."

"I'm glad I always bring my disinfectant with me." Bren tapped his Louie Vuitton satchel. "I also have a small can of Raid, just in case."

"Don't go all haywire with it," Derek croaked. "My lungs and your Lysol don't get along."

Bren pulled out the can. "Then I will only coat everything twice."

"Dudes, I'm so taking my shower first." Russ peeled off his T-shirt.

"We'd have it no other way, your Highness!" Bren mocked. "Just hurry up."

"Yeah, my skin's crawling, and the lungs are soon to follow," Derek stated. "When Bren is done fumigating, nothing will be alive after that."

Russ slid off his jeans. "Like, give me a couple of minutes to scrub off this grody stuff."

"A couple—being the key words," Derek countered. "And you better not lock the door either."

"We've two queen-sized beds." Bren unbuttoned his polo shirt. "I figured the Prince could have one to himself because he thrashes around all night and talks in his sleep. Not to mention the whole nudity thing."

"Okay." Derek agreed. "We'll take the other."

"Like, way cool." Russ jumped spread-eagle on the bed. "Who's your daddy?"

Bren looked at Derek. "What a freak."

He nodded. "Right!"

Bren wrung the excess liquid into a small cup and tightly squeezed the lid. "The guy who sold me this room asked why I was so wet."

"What did you tell him?" Derek slipped off his jeans.

Bren removed his leather belt. "A frat party that I attended went awry."

Russ crawled off the bed. "Like, I would've so stayed there and had me a rad time."

"What?" Bren asked.

"Imagine all the totally hot chicks that would've been there." Russ had his eyes closed.

Bren snapped his fingers. "Wake up, fool. It never took place."

Russ opened them and glared at him. "Dude, you're a major party pooper." He dropped his boxers to the floor, made a mad dash to the bathroom and slammed the door.

"We didn't need to see all that," Derek yelled.

"This place is already nasty enough without you adding to the mix," Bren screeched.

"Like, blow it out your ditty bags," Russ hollered out.

"If you don't hurry up, I'll come in and yank you out by your ditty bags," Bren roared back.

"You totally won't get in," Russ howled.

"What did I say about locking that door?" Derek shouted.

He heard the bathroom door being unlocked.

"Thank you."

"Like, whatever."

Derek took off his shirt. "I can't believe we fell into that container of liquid at Prescott Chemicals."

"You said that in the car a thousand times." Bren lowered his khakis. "If you're that afraid of heights then you shouldn't have looked down."

"I know." Derek sat on the bed and peeled off his socks. "It made me dizzy and I lost my balance. I'm sorry."

"You've also been down that road." Bren removed his Rolex watch. "We've already forgiven you so please, drop it."

"Okay, it's dropped." Derek took off his gold bracelet.

"I'm glad this is waterproof." Bren placed the timepiece on the nightstand.

"At least my twenty-four karat gold bracelet hasn't tarnished." Derek put it on the nightstand.

"That's a plus!"

"Yeah." Derek agreed. "I'm calling the shower next."

"I need to brush my teeth while you're washing," Bren said. "I've got an awful taste in my mouth. I swear I swallowed some of that solution."

"I was thinking that too." Derek grabbed his duffle bag. "I've got a funky taste all up in my mouth. I fell in head first."

Bren walked over and knocked on the bathroom door. "Hurry up in there. We need to take showers before we develop lesions on our skin or start balding."

Russ yelled back with toothpaste in his mouth. "Dude, maybe you'll get some mad blisters on your lips."

"Herpes is more your department," Bren bellowed.

Derek pushed by and pounded on the door. "C'mon, move it. We don't want this stuff on us any longer than we have to. We've no idea what it's doing to us or what harm it's causing."

"Like, totally come in." Russ rinsed the toothpaste from his mouth.

Derek opened the door. "Aw, man...he's naked."

"Slam it shut!" Bren turned his head askew. "My eyes are already burning and stinging."

"I'm giving you sixty seconds to come out with your towel covering your lower portion." Derek sneered as he counted down.

"He takes so much time in the bathroom," Bren stated. "My mother has never taken this long to bathe, apply makeup and dry her hair. And she's a society matron."

Russ finally came out with a towel wrapped around his waist. "That felt way awesome. I could've majorly stayed in there all night."

"Are you saying you didn't?" Bren snarled. "It certainly felt as if you did."

"Like, whatever," Russ retorted.

Derek escaped into the bathroom and closed the door.

"Are you in the shower?" Bren asked. "I want to brush my teeth."

"Like, you totally mean fangs," Russ muttered under his breath.

With a quick turn of the head, Bren threw him a vicious look.

"I just entered the shower," Derek yelled. "Come on in."

Russ winked. "Are you dudes taking a shower together?"

"Does your mind always have to be in the gutter?" Bren snapped.

"Only when my hot bod takes me there."

Bren opened the door. "You're impossible."

"I'm totally possible."

The bathroom door closed.

Russ felt warm, so he cranked the window slightly open. *Like, nobody could get in that small crack unless they were Spiderman.*

He took off his towel, walked toward the bed, slung it over the back of a chair and climbed naked under the sheets.

Russ grabbed the two pillows, stacked them on top of each other and slapped them for fluff.

After stretching out his hand, he picked up the remote control from the nightstand and noticed it had missing buttons. *Whoa, this thing totally needs a casket.*

Russ turned on the television, laid his head down and surfed the channels. He came upon his favorite, snuggled with his blanket and watched the show.

"That feels much better!" Derek exited the bathroom. He left the door and steam drifted out. "What're you watching?"

Russ beamed. "Skateboarding, dude!"

"Cool, I haven't watched that in a while."

Bren popped out his head. "Well, dudes, when I'm done shaving and moisturizing my handsome face, CNN is getting turned on so we can watch what's going on with the Woodbine case. There could be an update regarding Carlton's death."

Russ scrunched his face. "No way, man!"

"We'll see who gets his way when I come out," Bren declared.

"Like, yeah...out of the closet," Russ quipped.

"In your dreams," Bren countered.

"Girls, get a grip. School's ended, homework's done and lights out in five!" Derek ordered.

"Yes, sir!" Bren saluted then slammed shut the bathroom door.

"Who totally died and left you the boss?"

"You two did because you can't get along."

"He so wants to watch that rank news show."

"We need to watch CNN."

Russ cringed. "Ah, dude...really?"

"Really!" Derek nodded. "It is, after all, two against one."

"Like, remember this good deed." Russ tossed the control unit on the bed.

Derek picked it up. "Oh, I'll remember." He changed the channel and climbed under the blanket.

When Bren finished his nightly routine, he left the bathroom and climbed into bed.

"Did you get all your housekeeping done?" Derek chuckled.

"There's a major stain on that missing drawer." Russ pointed as he bared a grin.

"I'm bored with you two and your nonsense." Bren snatched the remote control from Derek's grasp and jumped from one news channel to another.

"Like, just pick one already," Russ declared.

Bren huffed. "All these stations are saying Carlton died from a drug overdose. At the same time they're poking sticks at the proverbial bear known as ACE with their asking why the group hasn't given any more information on the supposed cover-up."

Derek smirked. "That's all Jack needs is for them to get a second wind."

"I know," Bren remarked. "They'll be blustering the Woodbine cover-up all over again."

"Like, cover up your yap and find a cool jacked-up movie," Russ quipped.

Bren scowled as he clicked it over to the guide.

"Let's totally watch the monster truck rally."

"Not even close!" Bren spoke out. "Oh, look, Casablanca is on TCM with my two favorite actors, Humphrey Bogart and Ingrid Bergman."

"That's an awesome flick." Derek adjusted his pillow and sunk into it.

Russ sprawled out headfirst toward the foot of the bed and put his chin on folded arms.

"I cannot believe this!" Bren leaned back. "The stars must be in complete alignment tonight."

"Like, why?" Russ asked.

"We are all in agreement on something," Bren replied.

Derek smiled. "It's certainly looking that way."

Russ grinned. "Here's looking at you, kid."

They laughed as the show began.

When the 102 minute movie ended, Derek had fallen asleep and Russ' eyes were half-closed.

"That is the best picture!" Bren praised.

"It was totally rad." One eye had shut.

"Just once, I wish it was shown with the alternate ending I've heard about. Supposedly, Ingrid stays with Bogey and lets Paul fly off on his doomed mission."

As both eyes fell, out came the murmur, "That'd be way cool."

"Yes, it would be." Bren turned off the television, rolled over and went to snoozing.

A couple of hours later and with triumphant snoring sounds, Russ woke up feeling nauseous and achy, so he went into the bathroom, turned on the light and closed the door. A wooziness came over him.

I've so got to sit down. Once steadied over the toilet seat, he eased down and held his stomach tight. After some deep moaning and groaning, the cramps ushered forth.

I'm majorly sick. His face felt flush then started to burn, so Russ got up, looked into the mirror and saw several slight movements.

Like, I must have a fever. He brought a hand to his forehead. With stabbing pain, the arm once again cradled the belly. It began to convulse.

Ah, man, I'm going to hurl! As his mouth hung over the sink, the pangs of distress subsided.

Whoa, I hope this is way over. Russ brought his head up. When a visual hit the mirror, he noticed a change in his appearance. The facial features began to soften as his clipped sideburns and peach fuzz pulled into his skin. Curly, thick blonde hair cascaded past his condensing shoulders as the hands grew delicate nails. A ring that his grandfather gave him fell to the floor. He leaned against the sink with eyes closed as his insides trembled.

When I totally open my eyes, everything will be back to normal. He gradually opened them and stood back from the mirror that covered the entire upper wall. Russ' height marginally scaled. His torso became sensuous and the breasts began to grow as his stomach slimmed to reveal voluptuous hips. To his extreme surprise, the male organ reverted to form precise female genitalia. The legs became shapely as they slimmed down to narrow feet. He dropped to the floor with rapid breaths and pulled the bath mat over his face.

Like, this has to be a dream. After a couple of minutes, he lowered it and focused on the corner of the floor beside the tub. There sat his grandfather's ring. Russ quaked inside. That ring had never left his hand since the day it was put on. He grabbed the sink and yanked himself up, and with a swift lift of his head, looked into the mirror. Right in front of him stood—a woman.

As Russ shivered violently, an ear-piercing shriek that could break a champagne glass echoed forth. Amid a quick mid-turn away from the mirror, he lost his footing and brought down all the wet towels to the floor. As he laid there, another round of cramping ensued. This time with a prolonged groan.

Bren pounded on the bathroom door, and when no response was heard, Derek aided him in pushing it open. Under a heap of damp towels, Russ was curled up in the fetal position with his eyes shut.

"What is he doing with our towels?" Bren snatched them up and balked. "Yuck!" His head turned away. "He's naked."

"Why is he on the floor?" Derek lowered down. He shook him until his eyes opened.

"Like, where am I?" Russ was startled. "Whoa, my head hurts, dudes."

"I think you've been sleepwalking again." Derek replied.

"The last time that happened, you urinated in the kitchen garbage can," Bren noted. He sniffed the towels. "I don't smell anything funky." He hung up each one to dry.

Russ examined his body. "Like, I had such a mad nightmare!"

"Let's get you off this cold tile and into a warm bed." Derek grabbed his hand and helped him up. He wobbled and banged against Bren. Some towels fell off the shower rod.

"Will you stabilize him?"

"You could help me," Derek responded.

"I am, by hanging up our towels so we'll be able to take another shower in the morning," Bren groused. "This solution might still be in some cracks and crevices."

After he walked Russ toward the bed, Derek helped him under the covers and brought them up around his neck.

"There you go, you're all tucked in."

"Like, thanks for helping me."

"Why're you shaking?" Derek squeezed Russ' jittery hand.

"That grody nightmare felt so real." His emotions peaked. "Like, I'm still majorly rattled by it."

"Derek!"

Bren tossed something toward him.

He caught the item in mid-air then looked at it.

"I found it on the floor in the bathroom."

Derek's eyebrows creased. "Russ, I'm surprised you took this off."

"Like, what is it?"

"You're grandfather's ring."

Russ sat up as Derek handed it to him.

"I totally didn't!" His head shook.

"Maybe it slid off while you were showering," Derek suggested.

Russ shrugged. "Like, probably." His voice cracked.

"If you need anything, just give me a shout out." Derek turned around and hopped into his own bed.

Russ fell back into his pillows and stared at the large emerald as it danced against the light. His gramps gave it to him just before a rare cancer took the man's life. Both were born in the same month—May, to be exact—so he cherished it. With a strong shove, it was back on his finger.

Bren came out of the bathroom. "Well, everything in there is back to looking good."

"Good," Derek stated. "Now knock out that light so I can get some sleep."

Bren looked at Russ. "If you go for another darkened stroll through this rat trap, please try to hit the toilet. Even the sink would do. Just stay away from the shower. The only moistened towel I want to feel in the morning is the one that dried my showered body!" He shut off the lamp and climbed into bed.

Darkness consumed the room.

Like, was this a nightmare or a sleepwalk scare? Russ clutched his grandfather's ring.

Or maybe I hallucinated that rank mess because I'm way over tired. Russ raised the ring, took one last look at it then kissed it.

Grandpa, I totally miss you so much. A stray tear slid down his cheek as his lids fell lazy.

Like, what if this wasn't a dream. His eyes shot open.

Could this have majorly happened? He felt altered. *Will I totally turn into a woman again? And if so...when?*